The Sign of the
BLACK DAGGER

Joan Lingard

 Kelpies

Kelpies is an imprint of Floris Books

First published by Puffin Books, London in 2005
This edition published in 2014

© 2005 Joan Lingard
Map illustration by Paul Colicutt

The publisher acknowledges subsidy from
Creative Scotland towards the publication
of this volume

 This book is also available
as an eBook

British Library CIP data available
ISBN 978-178250-131-2
Printed in Poland

The Sign of the
BLACK DAGGER

For Rosa, Aedan, Shona and Amy

EDINBURGH

1796

PRINCES STREET

NORTH BRIDGE

(3.)

(4.)

Princes Street Gardens

HIGH STREET

SOUTH BRIDGE

(2.)

(1.)

GRASSMARKET

CHAMBER STREET

KEY:
1. EDINBURGH CASTLE
2. ST. GILES
3. ADVOCATE'S CLOSE
4. THE CROSS
5. CANONGATE TOLLBOOTH
6. CANONGATE CHURCH
7. WHITEHORSE CLOSE
8. HOLYROOD PALACE
9. ABBEY
10. *Madame de Polastran's* HOUSE

(10.)

(7.)

ABBEY STRAND

(5.)   (6.)   (8.)   (9.)

CANONGATE   HOLYROOD ROAD

COWGATE

Chapter 1

Lucy didn't like the look of the man the moment she opened the door. The light in the alley was dim and she couldn't see his face properly but the set of his shoulders and the angle of his head in some way intimidated her. She took a step back.

"I'm looking for Ranald Cunningham." He had a smooth voice but she didn't like it either.

"He's not in," she said.

"When will he be back?"

"I don't know."

"What about your mum?"

"She's at the library."

"Borrowing books?"

"No, she works there."

"When does she get back?"

"Just after eight. She works up on George IV Bridge."
Why had she told him that? Why was she telling him anything?

"And what about your dad? When does he usually get back?"

"Six. Half past, maybe. Not sure."

"It's gone six now. Can I come in and wait?"

Before she knew it he was inside. Her mother would be furious that she'd let a stranger come into the house. When Will asked her afterwards why she hadn't stopped him she said she hadn't known how to. He was that kind of man.

He followed her into the living room on the ground floor. Their house was a tall building on three floors, with not many rooms on each. Her school books were spread across the round table in the centre. She'd been doing her homework when the bell rang.

"Pretty old close this, eh? Did it not say fifteen something on the wall out there?"

"Fifteen ninety."

It also said: BLISSIT BE GOD ALMIGHTY OF AL HIS GIFTS. But she did not point that out.

"Walls must be all of three feet thick."

She was relieved when she heard Will's feet on the stairs. He pushed open the door and looked in.

"Will, this is someone for Dad."

"Cuthbert Smith, representing MacAtee, MacPherson

and Trimble." He produced a card from his top jacket pocket and presented it to Will. "Bert for short. No time for the Cuth bit." He seemed to think he'd made a joke.

Lucy looked at him stonily. She could see his face plainly now under the central ceiling light. It was very smooth and round and his shiny black hair was receding from the sides. He was a burly man, with wide shoulders and thick round the middle. He looked as if he had been poured into his clothes as he stood there with his feet planted wide apart.

Will was frowning as he studied the card. "MacAtee, MacPherson and Trimble, Financial Services," he read aloud. He looked up. "Is there a problem?"

"Can't talk business with you, son. Wouldn't be right. It's between me and your dad." He picked up a vase from the deep-set window sill and turned it upside down to examine the markings. "Pretty old too, from the look of it. Could be worth something, I imagine."

"Be careful!" cried Lucy as he made as if to drop it.

He smiled. "Gave you a fright, eh? Family heirloom?" He replaced it. "Your dad got a job?"

"Yes," said Lucy.

"He's self-employed," added Will.

"Doing what?"

"He's a consultant."

"What does he consult?"

"He advises people who want to set up businesses," said Will.

Mr Smith appeared to smirk. "A good businessman, is he?"

"We'll give him your card and tell him you called."

"I can wait for him." Mr Smith looked around for a chair but the cat was sleeping on an armchair on one side of the fireplace and Lucy had thrown her bag on the other.

"Can't be easy keeping this place warm," he remarked.

"I think you'd better come back another time." Will could be firm, and was now.

"Thing is, we've written him a few letters but he's never replied. What would you make of that?" He held out his hands, pudgy palms upward. "That's why I've been forced to make a house call. Would prefer not to have to, you understand. It's a perishing night to be out. There's a wind getting up."

They could hear it howling in the chimney. Lucy thought she had heard another noise, like that made by the front door opening. She turned her head. Perhaps it was their father arriving home. She couldn't be sure, though, with the moan of the wind masking noises outside the room.

"Don't know why people have to make things more

difficult for themselves than they need," Mr Smith went on, pulling back the cuff of his jacket to look at his watch. He sighed.

Lucy heard the door again, and this time she was sure that she had. It had closed with a click, but neither Will nor the man seemed to have registered it. She took a quick look into the hall. There was nobody there.

"Maybe I will come back later. What time did you say your mum gets in? Eight? I'll go and get myself a pint in the meantime. One thing about living on the Royal Mile, you're never far from a pub. Your dad visit the pubs, does he?"

"Sometimes," said Will.

"Got a favourite, has he?"

"Not that we know of."

And if we did we wouldn't tell you, thought Lucy.

Will showed the man out.

"See you later," he called back over his shoulder before he disappeared into the shadows of the narrow alleyway.

Will came back into the room.

"I've a feeling Dad must owe money," he said uneasily.

"I think he came back a few minutes ago."

"Who, Dad?" Will was startled.

Lucy nodded. "But then the door went again. Maybe he's been waiting outside till the man would leave."

Will couldn't imagine his father doing that but they went out to look anyway. They walked as far as the end of the close to where steps dropped down on to the street below. There was no sign of anyone lurking in the gloomy light.

The wind was strengthening and tugging at their clothes and whipping Lucy's long dark hair across her face. She shivered. "It's freezing out here. Let's go in, Will. He'll come back soon, I'm sure he will."

Their mother had left a note on the table in the morning with instructions about supper. At the appointed time they turned on the oven and twenty minutes later they put in the lasagne. Lucy cleared the table and Will set it with four places, as usual. They didn't talk any more about their father or the visitor.

At a quarter past eight their mother came in with her hair tossed and her cheeks glowing. "What a wind! I got you that book you wanted for your history project, Lucy."

"Thanks, Mum."

"Your father not back yet? He didn't say anything this morning about being late. Oh well, something must have come up. He hasn't phoned?"

"I'll try him on his mobile, shall I?" Lucy jumped up and went to the phone. She dialled, and waited. "It's ringing."

Will frowned. "I think I can hear it ringing up the

stairs." He dashed up and came down with the mobile in his hands.

Their mother shook her head. "That probably explains it!"

Will clicked the mobile off and put it on the dresser. He then lifted Cuthbert Smith's card and laid it on the table in front of his mother. "This man was looking for Dad."

Their mother put on her glasses to read the card. "Never heard of them. Probably trying to talk your father into a loan. These sharks are everywhere, on the telly, on the phone! Trying to tempt people to borrow more than they can afford. It's a scandal."

As she spoke the phone rang. Lucy leapt on it. "Hello," she said, "this is the Cunningham house." Her voiced tailed away and then she said, "I'm sorry, we're not interested," which was what her parents had told her to say when someone was either trying to sell something or bringing the glad tidings that they had won a prize. She replaced the receiver. "Double glazing."

"As if we could double-glaze these windows!" said their mother cheerfully. She remained cheerful throughout the meal though Lucy and Will found it difficult to be. Their eyes kept going to their father's empty place.

"He wasn't a very nice man, Mr Smith," said Lucy.

"I'm sure he wasn't. I don't know what possessed you to let him in in the first place."

They finished their meal and Lucy cleared up, it being her turn. They had a dishwasher so there was not a great deal to do. By half past nine, the time they normally went to bed on school nights, their mother was beginning to sound a little worried.

"I'm surprised he hasn't phoned by now. He could surely have found a telephone box somewhere."

Just then, the doorbell rang.

"That might be our man back again," said Will, springing up.

"I'll go," said their mother.

Will followed her into the hall and stood behind her while she opened the door to reveal Cuthbert Smith standing on the step. Will tried to make himself look bigger as the man began to talk in a menacing manner to his mother.

"I'm very sorry, Mr Smith," she said politely, cutting him off, "but my husband is not at home and I am unable to help you. I suggest you phone him at his office."

"I've tried all that, writing, phoning. Answer machine's always on."

"I'm afraid I am unable to help you. Goodnight, Mr Smith." He had his foot over the step. She stared down at it until he removed it.

"Tell him he'll not get away with it!" he shouted as the door was closed in front of him.

"I see what you mean," said their mother. "He isn't a very nice man."

By now she was looking troubled and when the phone rang she answered it herself.

"Oh hello, Mum," she said, her voice flat. "No, no, I'm fine. I'm just tired." Their gran was always fussing about their mother's health. "No, we're all fine. There's nothing wrong." They chatted for a few minutes, during which their mother fiddled with the phone cord and glanced at her watch. Eventually she said, "Hope to see you soon," and replaced the receiver.

At ten o'clock, she said firmly, "It's time you were away to bed."

"I want to wait till Dad comes in," said Lucy.

"He's probably met someone." Their mother did not sound convinced.

At eleven o'clock, she was trying to take refuge in annoyance. "Really, this is too bad of Ranald! Go to bed, Lucy! Will! You'll never get up in the morning."

They made no move.

"Mum," said Will, "don't you think Dad's been acting a bit funny recently?"

"What do you mean *funny*?"

"Well, not himself. As if he's far away half the time.

Sometimes when you speak to him he doesn't seem to hear."

Their mother sighed. "You're right, I've thought so myself. But you know what he's like – if you ask him if there's anything wrong he says he's fine."

"Just like you, Mum," said Lucy.

Her mother gave her a black look.

At midnight, Will said, "Do you not think we should phone the police?"

"The police? It's not come to that. I'm sure he'll be back by morning."

Will was first up. There was no sign of his father. He went to the phone and stood staring at it, willing it to ring. It didn't. Alongside lay the message pad. His father had been doodling again. He always doodled while he talked on the phone. Will bent his head to take a closer look. The page was scrawled all over with drawings in black pen. He had hoped he might find a clue but he couldn't make much sense of any of it. The same motif occurred over and over again: an upright with a shorter stroke across it, near the top. He tore the page off and turned as Lucy came in yawning, her hair tousled.

"What's that?" she asked.

"Just Dad doodling again." He showed her.

She shrugged and went to fill the kettle. The first

thing their mum wanted in the morning was a cup of tea. She always said she didn't feel human until she had one.

When she appeared they saw from the blue shadows under her eyes that she had scarcely slept at all. Not that they had done too much sleeping themselves. Lucy couldn't stop yawning. She announced that she was not going to school.

"You have to," her mother replied listlessly, staring over the rim of her cup into space.

"I'm not, not until I know Dad's all right."

"He could have had an accident," said Will. "Or been taken ill."

"But surely somebody would have phoned us," said their mother.

"Unless he's unconscious and not able to tell them our address."

"He'd have his wallet on him, with his cards in it."

"Somebody could have mugged him," put in Lucy, "and stolen his wallet."

They were not very inclined to believe any of these propositions. Nevertheless, their mother decided to phone the Accident and Emergency departments at the two major hospitals and ask if anyone resembling her husband had been brought in. No one had, which did not surprise them.

By this time it was too late for the children to go

to school. At half past nine, their mother phoned his office; not that they really thought he would be there when he hadn't been home. But his secretary Pauline should be, and she might have some idea.

The answering machine was on. "Hi," said their father's voice, full of life, "this is Ranald Cunningham here. Sorry, can't speak to you right now, but please leave a message."

They didn't leave one.

"Funny Pauline's not there," said Will.

"He wouldn't have run off—" began Lucy and then stopped. She had been going to say that her father wouldn't have run off with Pauline, would he? The father of one of her friends had run off with his secretary.

"Don't be stupid," snapped Will.

The phone rang and Lucy beat him to it.

"Good morning," said the smooth voice, "this is Bert Smith. Remember I paid you a little call yesterday evening regarding a bit of business with your father? I wonder if he would be at home now?"

"I'm afraid not."

"You're afraid not? He's not in his office, either. Have you seen him since last night?" When Lucy did not answer he said, "Done a bunk, has he?"

"Give me the phone, Lucy." Her mother took the receiver from her. "I'm sorry, Mr Smith but, as I told you yesterday, I cannot be of any help." She put down the phone and turned to them. "If he's not back by the time I come home from work tonight I'll phone the police."

Lucy felt uneasy about that. "What if he's in trouble? What if he's done something wrong? He wouldn't, would he, Mum?"

"I don't know, dear. I hope not. But I just don't know. You think you know someone—" She stopped.

After lunch, their mother went to work, having given them instructions to do some schoolwork and not waste the entire afternoon. But they found it hard to settle down. They became edgy with each other. Lucy put on a CD; Will said it was too loud. It was not long before they had a proper spat. Lucy knocked over her half-full mug of hot chocolate which trickled as far as Will's history jotter.

"Look what you've done, idiot!"

"I couldn't help it."

"Yes, you could. You just don't look."

"And you're so wonderful, aren't you? What about last week when you dropped the egg box?"

Will grunted and opened the jotter, which now had brown edges to its pages, and picked up his pen, though he didn't begin to write. He said, "I'm worried about Dad."

"Do you think I'm not?"

Lucy got up and wandered about. She stopped by the wall, near the fireplace, and fingered the rough stone. These walls had stood for centuries and sheltered all their ancestors. What if the house had to be sold to pay Mr Smith?

"Ouch!" she exclaimed suddenly and put her index finger in her mouth. It was bleeding a little.

"What have you done now?"

"Lot of sympathy I get from you. There's a sharp edge there on the stone. It's sticking out a bit." She bent her head to look more closely. Tentatively she touched it again. "I think there's a loose stone."

"Wouldn't be surprising, I suppose, after all these years. Watch you don't cut yourself again."

Lucy paid no attention. She was concentrating on trying to move the stone.

"What are you doing taking the place apart?"

If their mother were to walk in now she'd have a fit. She'd ask Lucy if she couldn't leave anything alone. From the moment she could crawl Lucy had always stuck her nose into everything.

"It's coming out," she said excitedly.

Will got up and went to join her. He put his hands underneath the stone alongside hers and together they began to lever it out from the wall. No daylight could be seen in the vacuum; there was another stone behind this one.

"I think we should put it back," said Will, "in case the wall starts to collapse."

"No, I can see something!"

They lowered the stone to the floor and Lucy thrust her arm into the opening. "There's something here!"

She brought out a dusty parcel wrapped in oilcloth. They sneezed. The dust of centuries must be coated on it. Their hands collided as they feverishly unwrapped the package. Lying in the middle of the dirty oilcloth was a cloth-bound book. It might once have been blue or green but was now almost colourless.

"Goodness!" cried Lucy, lifting it up.

"Be careful. It might fall to pieces."

They opened it gingerly. Facing them, on the front page, was a black-ink drawing of a dagger.

"Let's see what's inside," said Lucy.

"A dagger!" cried Will. He pulled the piece of paper his dad had doodled on from his pocket. "Don't they look like daggers to you?"

"I suppose they might." Lucy considered the drawings, her head cocked to one side. "But I'm not sure. You might just think that because of the dagger here. I mean, why would Dad draw *daggers*?"

"I don't know." Will shrugged. "Let's see what's in the book."

The pages were yellowed with age and spotted with brown stains but the handwriting was still clearly visible. It was well formed, elegant handwriting with curves and loops; not like the scrawls they tended to do. They read the title page.

The journal of Louisa and William Cunningham, begun on the sixth day of January, 1796, and completed on the thirty-first day of the same month in the same year.

"William and Louisa!" exclaimed Lucy. "The same names as ours." They had always known that they'd been given family names, though they had shortened theirs. "Isn't that strange? I wonder if they could be twins?" Like themselves.

They read on.

We have taken it in turns to write this account. It is the story of our father, Ranald Cunningham, and what befell him in January of this year, 1796.

"Ranald Cunningham!" exclaimed Will.
Lucy turned over the page.

Chapter 2

Louisa

We were so disturbed by the events of today, Wednesday, January the sixth, 1796, that we have decided to begin this journal. My twin brother William says it may be a way to help us understand our confused thoughts about our father and what has befallen him.

The day began well, even though the morning was cold and grey, with a bitter wind blowing off the sea. We had gone early down to the port of Leith with our parents to watch the arrival of Charles-Philippe, the Comte d'Artois. We went early since large crowds were expected. The count is the brother of the French King Louis XVI, who was so cruelly executed in Paris three years ago. His head was chopped off at the guillotine while the crowd watched. It was said they cheered when it fell and some old women sat knitting throughout. We were sad when we heard the news, our mother especially, for she is French herself. Some months afterwards, his queen Marie Antoinette suffered the same fate. So now France is a republic and the royals have all been banished or fled. That is why the Comte d'Artois has come to Scotland.

"Stay close beside us," warned our father. Some in the crowd were pushing and shoving. One woman had stepped right in the middle of my foot and paid no attention when I cried out. Everyone was anxious to get a glimpse of the count's court. Our father pointed out Lord Adam Gordon who was waiting on the pier with his coach ready to convey the count up to Edinburgh. Unfortunately, with Lord Adam being in mourning due to the death of his wife, the coach had been painted black. It did not look very cheerful, with the four long-tailed sable horses waiting to draw it.

"I hope it will not bring bad luck." Our mother shivered, then added, "Put your coat collars up, *mes enfants*." She is always anxious about draughts and cold winds. She finds Edinburgh's east wind very chilly. She lived in the south of France as a girl where the wind was warm and smelled of lavender. Whereas here, she says, our streets smell like sewers.

At two o'clock, His Majesty's frigate, *Jason*, came sailing into the port, with the guns of the Leith Battery firing off a twenty-one gun salute. The noise was deafening. I had to put my fingers in my ears. When it had finished and the smell of gunpowder hung in the air the crowd cheered, us amongst them.

Since we were near the front we had a good view of the count and his friends. He smiled and raised his cocked hat in response to the people's welcome. He looked very fine in his frock coat with epaulettes on the shoulders, and his tight knee breeches. His boots, too, were tight-fitting, and one could tell that the leather would be soft and supple. As he came down the gangway on to the pier we saw that he sported a large eight-pointed star on his left chest. It was the star of Saint Esprit, our mother told us.

"He is known as *le beau Artois*. The handsome Artois."

She had not needed to translate for we can speak French passably, William and I. Our mother speaks English with a strong French accent, sometimes making wild mistakes. Until the Revolution and the overthrow of the French monarchy she was longing to return to France. She no longer does; not that she would be in danger herself for we are not aristocrats. Our father is a scholar and he does not earn a great deal of money, which was one of the reasons that our troubles were about to begin.

The count was followed off the ship by a long train of friends and supporters, men and women, *emigrés* like himself, dukes and duchesses amongst them. The ladies were richly dressed, in silk, satin and velvet. They had to hold on to their plumed hats when the frisky Leith wind tried to lift them from their heads. They took it well, however. They laughed. The chatter of French voices reached us and made our mother smile. She looks radiant when she smiles. It is as if the sun has come out.

"Look at that red velvet frock, Ranald," she said, pointing to a very elegant-looking lady. "And are their wigs not fine? I should so love a velvet dress of that colour. It would make me feel warm to wear it."

"Then you shall have one as soon as I can afford it, Anne-Marie," our father responded, touching her arm affectionately. He would give her the moon if he could find a ladder long enough to climb up and reach it.

"And when will that be?" She pouted a little. She loves beautiful clothes.

"As soon as my book is published."

"And do you think a publisher is going to pay you very much for that?"

"I am hoping so."

"You are such an *optimiste*, Ranald!"

That is one of the things we like about our father. He always looks on the bright side. We know, of course, that he is impractical, and that often makes life difficult for our mother. And, as we were soon to find out, for us too.

The new arrivals climbed into the carriages waiting on the dockside and set off up the hill towards the palace. We turned our footsteps there too, though we must go on foot. It is a long walk, some three miles or so, but our father believes in fresh air and long walks. He says it will make us grow up healthy and strong. Certainly William is strong and, at thirteen, as tall as many men. He is much taller than me, of course, even though we are the same age.

As we moved away our father greeted a man who had also been watching the royal departure.

"*Bonjour*, Monsieur Goriot," said our father, raising his hat.

"*Bonjour*, Monsieur Cunningham." He pronounced our surname in the way a Frenchman with poor English might.

He went ahead of us.

It was strange but I had not cared for the man's face, even from that brief glimpse. It was pockmarked, which he could not help, of course, but there had been something sly in his look and I was surprised that Papa knew such a man. Our father, though, is a very friendly person and will talk to anyone. William says I make up my mind too quickly about people and perhaps that is true but I often find that I am right once I get to know them. He agrees with me, however, that our father is not a great judge of character.

"A Frenchman?" said our mother, taking hold of our father's arm as we set off up the hill. She'd been complaining that her shoes cramped her feet and that she needed new ones. These had been cheap and not very comfortable from the start.

"An *emigré*," said our father. "I've occasionally passed the time of day with him when we've met in a tavern."

"As long as you have not lent him any monies!" Our mother was only half joking. Our father is not good when it comes to managing his finances. He has his head in the clouds half the time; I cannot think of any better way to describe it.

"Only the odd crown," he replied.

"*Only?*"

"Don't worry, my love. He will pay me back."

To change the conversation and avoid a row, William asked our father why the count had come to live in the Palace of Holyroodhouse.

"To seek Sanctuary."

We knew that debtors sought Sanctuary in the palace's abbey and its grounds, under an ancient privilege asserted by the abbots. There, they cannot be arrested and, from midnight Saturday until midnight Sunday, they are free to leave and go where they wish. But if they are caught outside even one minute late they can be arrested by the messenger-at-arms and put in jail. We have often seen debtors fleeing down the High Street on a Sunday night with the messenger after them brandishing his ebony wand with its silver tip. It is called a Wand of Peace – a strange name, is it not, for a wand that brings misery? He must tap the debtor on the shoulder with it before he can arrest him. It is a bit like the game of tag, only more serious.

"Surely the messenger man would not be permitted to *touch* the Comte d'Artois with that black stick of his!" Our mother was scandalised at the very thought.

"He would, I'm afraid, my dear."

"Does he owe very much?"

"I heard more than two million francs."

"There must be mistake. I do not believe he is criminal." Our mother speaks English in her own fashion.

"No one has said he is, my dear. He has just been unfortunate."

"Or not very good at looking after money," said William.

As we were nearing the top of Leith Walk, Papa suggested taking a detour round by the abbey. Normally our mother would have protested at the idea of lengthening our walk but she was as eager as we were to see what we could of the French royal party. We took a low road, which brought us out almost to the gates of Holyrood.

The whole area was abuzz. It was as if there was a fair going on. Carriages and coaches stood in the roadway and the courtyard. Children pranced about, trying to touch the horses, and even dive underneath them, and were being shouted at by the drivers. "Ye'll git yersel's kilt!" Hawkers were offering their wares. Bootlaces, pretty ribbons, combs for one's hair. We saw Monsieur Goriot again but he did not see us. And all the while servants were running in and out of the houses clustered around the abbey and the palace. Our father told us that the owners often take in debtors as lodgers who are then known as 'abbey lairds'. That is something of a joke as a laird is normally a man of means.

Beyond the abbey lies Holyrood Park, in the middle of which stands the hill that we call Arthur's Seat. I was thinking that debtors who cannot pay for lodging may have to lodge out in the open park. The thought made me shiver.

We stopped at the Abbey Strand so that our father could point out the three brass letters SSS spaced across the roadway. They mark the boundary of the abbey precincts and of the sanctuary.

"So the count will have to get his feet over this line before midnight on Sundays. Otherwise he might be pursued by his creditors down the High Street until the last second, hoping that he might trip and fall!"

We thought it amusing, then.

We crossed the road, skirted the Girth Cross, and were in the burgh of Canongate, which adjoins the High Street, where we live, opposite St Giles Cathedral, in Advocate's Close. I had to stop to tighten the laces of my right boot. I gave William my muff to hold while I did so. As I was putting one hand against the wall to steady myself I felt some deep cuts in the stone. When I had finished with my boot I examined the wall.

"What is it?" asked William.

"Someone's been cutting something into the stone." I bent to examine it more closely. "It looks like a symbol. It looks rather like a dagger."

William shrugged and we carried on up the Canongate, which boasts several fine mansions. William and I went ahead, for our mother's steps were slowing and it was beginning to spit with rain. I kept my hands tucked deep into my fur muff now. It was a Christmas present from Papa and I loved the warmth of it.

Once we left the Canongate behind and were in the High Street, which is lined with high stone tenements, there were more people to be seen. Ragged, barefoot children were scuttling around in spite of the cold. Rich and poor live cheek-by-jowl here, as our father puts it; the poor living, as would be expected, in lesser dwellings, often no more than hovels. Many houses are divided into smaller parts. We are fortunate ourselves to live in a whole one since our father inherited it from his father, who inherited it from his father.

One tiny girl came running up to us, cupping her mottled, purple hands and holding them out to us, beseeching us with the look in her eyes, for she did not speak. Green snot ran from her nostrils. I desperately wished that I could lend her my muff, even for a few minutes, so that she could warm those hands, but I only had one and there was a number of children. Once I had given my scarf to a girl and started a riot. In the end the scarf was tugged to pieces so Papa said it would not be advisable to do that again. He and our mother were kind to the children, though. They did not give them money for they said that the children's parents would take it and spend it on gin, but they always told Bessie to give them hot soup or a bannock whenever they came to the door.

We hoped Bessie would have the kettle boiling now, with scones still warm from the griddle. My mouth began to water at the thought of them. The long walk had made us ravenous.

The girl was keeping pace with us. I searched in my pocket and found a sweet, a clove ball. I put it into her hand, and also my lace-edged handkerchief, one of a number sent to me by my grandmother in France. She put the clove ball into her mouth quickly before another child could snatch it. The sweet bulged in the side of her cheek. But she did not wipe her nose. She ran off with the handkerchief, waving it over her head like a trophy.

We turned into our close and stopped dead at the top of the steps. The alley drops steeply downward. The tenements on either side are tall with jutting timber projections, which means that the light is poor, especially on a winter day. We were just able to discern two men outside our door. The way they were standing there suggested trouble. As we went slowly down the steps to meet them we saw that one of them was dressed in greenish-black clothes, while the other wore livery bearing the royal coat of arms.

"This your house?" asked the one in black. He had an oily voice that matched his greasy clothes.

"It is," said William.

"We are looking for Mr Ranald Cunningham."

We saw then that the messenger-at-arms was holding an ebony wand with a silver tip.

At that same moment, our parents arrived at the close-head.

"Run, Papa, run!" shouted William.

Our father ran.

Chapter 3

"You can't still be put in prison for debt, can you?" asked Lucy anxiously, looking up from the journal.

"I don't think so, but I'm not sure," said Will. "Depends on the debt, perhaps. If it involves fraud. But they don't have special debtors' prisons any more, I do know that." He thought he might like to be a lawyer when he grew up.

"It must have been horrible for them when their father had to run."

"And awful for him too," Will added. "I expect he felt guilty."

"He must have owed a lot of money."

They were silent, thinking about their own father. Where *on earth was he?* The abbey sanctuary no longer existed. It belonged to a time long past.

"Mum'll be coming in soon," said Lucy. "We'd better try to get some food ready." She had left no instructions today.

"Shall we put the book back for now?" suggested Will.

"Yes, let's."

They wanted it to be their secret though neither said so. They often didn't need to tell each other what they were thinking. After they'd cleaned the oilcloth as best they could, they rewrapped the book and tucked it into the hole in the wall and replaced the stone. Then they had to scrub their hands, which were filthy.

They rummaged in the cupboard and brought out whatever they could find. Will was a better cook than Lucy so he took charge. He chopped up onions, peppers and mushrooms and put some rice on to boil. He was going to make a risotto; something he had never done before but had watched his father do. Lucy set the table.

When their mother arrived home, she said, "He's not back?" She shook her head. "I don't know what to do. I've phoned one or two people but they've not seen him. It's beginning to look like he is trying to avoid Mr Smith." She stopped. "What's the smell?" she asked.

Will had burnt the rice but most of it turned out to be edible, more or less, and none of them was in the least bothered about what they ate. Their mother decided to have a glass of red wine with hers and allowed them to have a glass of half wine and half water.

"I need something to perk me up a bit," she said as she poured the wine. "And after we've eaten I suppose I should phone the police."

Will and Lucy still felt uneasy about that. What if their father had done something illegal? They could hardly bear to think that he would have done but what if he *had*? Ringing the police would be like tipping them off. Imagine ratting on your own father!

"Maybe we should wait another day?" suggested Will.

Maybe they should, agreed their mother. Anyway, they kept thinking that he would turn up any moment now and wonder what all the fuss was about. Hadn't he told them he was going to Aberdeen for the night on business? He'd say.

"You're sure he didn't mention having business outside Edinburgh?" asked Will.

"He hasn't been out of town for ages. Not as far as I know."

As they were finishing their meal, the doorbell rang. Will went to answer it.

It was Mr Smith, back yet again, this time with another man for company. Will thought the second one looked like a bouncer he'd seen standing outside the door of a club in the Cowgate.

"I'm sorry," he said straight away, "our father is not at home."

"Are we supposed to believe that?" Mr Smith's voice was not as smooth as it had been the day before. "Sure he's not holed up inside trying to avoid us? It's cold out here. Can't imagine him not wanting to get into the warm."

Their mother came out into the lobby. "I've told you, Mr Smith—"

He cut across her. "I know what you've told me, dear. But there's something funny going on, if you ask me. Either you know where your husband is or you don't. And if you don't, we might have to see if there are other ways to find him. He owes us a lot of dosh. So now it seems he's run off and left you all high and dry."

He had his foot planted firmly over the threshold again and the other man had moved up closer.

"If you don't leave us alone, I'll have to call the police."

"Do that then. Call them! Save us the bother of doing it ourselves."

Suddenly, Will gave Mr Smith a push in the chest and quickly closed and bolted the door.

"I don't know if that was wise," said his mother as the men hammered on the door, cursing them. Fortunately, the door was stout.

"I don't care. We had to get rid of them."

"They'll be back, though, I'm afraid."

Again, they all passed a restless night.

In the morning, which was Saturday, they sat round the table not eating their breakfast and discussing what they should do.

"Why don't we go round to the office," said Will, "and see if there's anything there that would give us a clue?"

Their mother had a key and the office was only a few minutes' walk away. There was some mail in the entrance lobby at the back of the door; not much, mostly trash mail and catalogues. Their mother opened the two white envelopes amongst them. One was from MacAtee, MacPherson and Trimble, demanding immediate payment for fifty thousand pounds.

"What?" gasped Will. "Fifty *thousand*!"

Their mother had turned pale. This was much worse than they'd imagined, not that they'd thought of any actual amount their father might owe. The second letter had red headings and was from the telephone company announcing that if the current bill was not settled immediately the telephone would be cut off.

They went through to the office. The two rooms had an abandoned air but perhaps that was because the computers and photocopier were covered in plastic and everything, including the two telephones, sat on the desk tops looking as if they had not been disturbed for a long time. The desk drawers and the filing cabinets were locked and there was no sign of keys. The wastepaper baskets had not been emptied but apart from that the room was amazingly tidy, which surprised them, considering that their father was basically untidy. They had no sense of his ever having been here.

"Odd," said their mother, running her hand along the secretary's desk top. "I thought the cleaner would have been in." She regarded the skim of dust lying on her hand.

In the top drawer of the secretary's desk, they found a telephone book.

"Why don't we phone Pauline?" said Lucy, flipping through it. "Her home number's here."

She dialled the number and handed over the receiver when Pauline answered. It was an awkward call for their mother to make.

"I was just wondering, Pauline, if Ranald said anything about having to make a trip somewhere this week?"

Lucy crossed two fingers and held them in the air. Will gazed out of the window, seeing nothing.

Their mum was frowning while she listened to what Pauline was saying at the other end of the line. "Oh, I see. I didn't know. Well, no, he didn't actually say anything."

"What is it, Mum?" asked Lucy, unable to bear the suspense.

"Shush, love." Their mother listened again and then said, "I'm very sorry about that, Pauline. Fifteen hundred pounds, did you say? I'll send you a cheque straight away. I'm really terribly sorry." She put the receiver down and stared straight ahead.

"What did she say?" cried Lucy.

"He paid Pauline off three months ago. Well, he didn't actually pay her off. He owed her fifteen hundred pounds in wages. He said he'd send it as soon as he could. He hasn't sent it."

"Fifteen hundred pounds," echoed Will. "Where will you get it?"

"I've still got some of Aunt Mary's money left." Their great-aunt had died the year before and left their mother a small inheritance. "But not enough to pay those loan sharks fifty thousand."

Will was tugging at the desk drawers but they were all locked. "There must be keys around somewhere. You'd think he'd leave a set in the office." He wandered off to have a look.

He searched underneath both desks and filing cabinets, checked the first-aid cabinet in the toilet and the cupboard in the tiny kitchen, which held two mugs, a tin of instant coffee and half a packet of digestive biscuits. They looked soggy. They might have been left behind by Pauline.

He went back to the entrance lobby and, looking up,

his eye caught sight of the electricity meter box. He reached up, opened it and found a set of keys.

They fitted the filing cabinets and the desk drawers. In the top drawer of their father's desk they found his diary. They leafed back over the last few weeks. The pages were absolutely blank.

"Why didn't he talk to me?" said their mother.

In the bottom drawer they found bills. Dozens of them, in brown envelopes. Some had not even been opened. Amongst them were long white envelopes which held statements from both bank and credit card companies.

Their father had been running his credit and overdraft allowances to the limit and paying off small sums every month, enough to keep the companies happy but, meanwhile, interest had been steadily increasing on the amounts left unpaid. He now owed all of them huge sums of money. He'd spent a lot over Christmas especially, they saw. For presents, for them.

"Why did he do all that?" cried Lucy.

"The business was obviously not working out." Their mother banged her fist down on the desk. "If only he'd *told* me. I suppose he started borrowing in a small way, hoping things would get better and he'd be able to pay off his debts."

"But they snowballed," said Will.

"Yes, you could say that." Their mother let the bills trickle through her fingers. "He always looks on the bright side; thinks his ship is about to come in!"

"It would need to be a pretty big ship," said Lucy, and for a moment they smiled.

Chapter 4

William

We brought our mother into the house and Bessie fetched the smelling salts. Our father is fleet of foot and lean of build. The two men who had come to arrest him were not. The one with the ebony wand had puffed heavily as he had tried to run up the steps to the top of the close and the other had wasted his breath by uttering cries, such as, "I'll get you, Cunningham. You won't escape me."

I had not stopped to think before I shouted, "Run, Papa, run!" Nor do I think that our father had stopped to consider, either, before he ran. But I believe it was the right thing to do. At least, if he took refuge in Sanctuary for a while he would have time to think. About what? Debts, I supposed.

That was what had jumped into my mind straight away. I had been wondering for some time how our father could keep plying our mother with gifts when there was little sign of any money coming in. A small amount was paid to him monthly from an inheritance trust but we knew it was not very much. Our mother kept telling us so.

She was having hysterics now that she had come out of her swoon. "Help me loosen her stays, Louisa," cried Bessie. "She can hardly breathe. She will have me draw her waist in until I fear for her organs." It is obvious that Bessie herself does not wear corsets; we can see that. It is something that I am not supposed to notice, but I do. She allows herself to spread comfortably. "And ye, William, be a guid lad and fetch yer puir mither some brandy."

I went upstairs to the drawing room and poured a measure of brandy into a glass. As I turned to go back down, Louisa came in.

"I do not intend to wear corsets," she announced, which she might be expected to do in a year or two. "I *hate* the thought of having my body squashed in like that. It's no wonder Maman could hardly breathe. As soon as we loosened the laces you could see she was relieved."

"I expect you will change your mind when the time comes."

Louisa tossed her dark curls, which our mother has persuaded her to wear in ringlets. "I certainly will not!"

She plumped up the cushion on the chaise longue and took a tartan blanket from the cupboard. "Maman is coming up to lie down."

She came in on Bessie's arm, the hysterics having given way to sighing. Bessie and Louisa made her comfortable on the sofa and I handed her the brandy. She sipped and seemed to feel a little better.

"What have we done to suffer this misfortune?" she cried. "*Mon Dieu!* May He remove us from this! How did that nasty little man come to have a – what do you call it?"

"A warrant, Mam," supplied Bessie.

"For my poor Ranald's arrest? He has not done wrong." The rest of us were silent.

"What is it all about?" she demanded.

"Debts," said Bessie, folding her hands in front of her stomach.

"*Debts?*"

"Yes, Mam. I fear so."

"Why do you think that, Bessie?"

"They are all stuffed inside the bureau."

"Have you been prying into your master's papers?"

"No, Mam. One day, when I was dustin' – I ken ye like the place kept nice and clean – the lid fell doon and oot they tumbled. Look, I'll show ye."

She went to the bureau and pulled down the lid and out came a shower of papers. Louisa and I did not make any move yet to pick them up.

"How did you know they were bills, Bessie?" asked our mother. "You cannot read."

"I ken tell when there's numbers wrote all over a paper. Look like bills tae me."

They looked like bills to us too.

"Go finish the cooking, Bessie. *Allez! Vite!* And close the door behind you."

"Yes, Mam."

When the door was closed, our mother said, "I shall have to give her a sack. She had no rights to look inside the bureau."

"You can't do that," objected Louisa. "She's been with the family forever."

"Besides," I said, "I think Papa owes her wages."

"Wages! She doesn't need wages. We have given her bed and board all these years. She has wanted for nothing."

"Papa would be angry if you sacked her." I thought it very unlikely that she would do it. She needs Bessie too much.

"He is not in position to be angry now, is he? What is he going to do?" She threw up her hands. "Where will he sleep? On the grass in the park? Tell me that!"

We could not tell her.

She continued. "They won't take him in the palace. He is not a noble. He is only a poor scholar. Your *grandmère* was against my marriage from the start. She said I would do better to marry an honest tradesman with a thriving business than a scholar. Especially a Scotch scholar! A leather merchant in our town wished for me to marry him."

"It's too late now," I said.

"When you come to choose a husband, Louisa, take my advice and do not allow the heart to be the rule of the head. You, too, William, with a wife." On another day she is liable to tell us that love matters more than anything else in life.

"Should we pick up the bills?" I asked.

"We can't let them lie for all the world to see."

"All the world doesn't come in here," said Louisa.

"Oh, you children can be tiresome at times!" Our mother threw up her hands again. It is one of her favourite gestures.

Louisa and I went down on our knees and began to scoop up the pieces of paper. There were bills for hats and gowns, boots and shoes, jewels and trinkets, and one for a fur muff.

"That must be my muff," cried Louisa. "I shall take it back to the shop."

"You can't do that!" Our mother was horrified. "It would be too embarrassing."

I thought it would be more embarrassing not to pay for it but I did not say so. Our mother was in no state to be challenged.

"What will we do with them?" I asked, my hands full of the unpaid bills.

"Put them back in the bureau and lock it! I don't know why your father leave it unlocked."

"He doesn't think to lock things up."

"It would be better for us if he did."

We did as our mother requested and I gave her the key. She sighed. "My poor Ranald. If only he didn't spend so much time reading! He'll freeze to death if he stay all night in the park."

"He can't come home till Sunday," Louisa pointed out.

"I'll take a blanket," I said, "and go and see if I can find him."

"I'll go with you." Louisa jumped up.

"Ask Bessie to give you some soup and a couple of bannocks. And be careful on the street! It will be getting dark soon. It gets dark so early in this northern country."

"But the nights are long and light in summer," countered Louisa.

"It is a long time till summer," sighed our mother. "Give your papa my love."

We left her to sip her brandy and went down to the kitchen to ask Bessie for a blanket and nourishment for our father.

"He'll need a' he can get, puir soul," she said as she ladled soup into a milk can. "He doesne live in this world, that's his trouble. His heid's aye in the clouds. Wrap up warm now, the twa' of ye."

We always do what Bessie tells us. She gave us

instructions about watching out for footpads, beggars and drunk men. "Dinne hing aroun' too long. I want to see ye hame afore the light fails."

It was failing now, and almost dark in the close. The street itself was lighter once we reached it and we were glad to see signs of a half-moon coming up. We hastened down the hill, Louisa taking care not to slop the soup. I carried the heavy blanket, two bannocks and a lump of cold mutton. It was still drizzling slightly.

We crossed the sanctuary line and were in the Abbey Strand. The taverns still seemed to be busy judging by the din coming from them but our father would not have money to spend on ale. We could see no sign of him in the Strand and since he could not be in any of the houses we thought that he might be in the park. But the park is large. It stretches as far as the village of Duddingston and is said to measure four miles round the perimeter.

We stood, undecided. I thought he must have gone to try to find some cover.

"What about St Anthony's Chapel?" suggested Louisa.

The ancient chapel is a ruin but it would offer a little shelter from the wind and rain. We had gone there with our father on several occasions to admire the view over the town to the Firth of Forth and the Kingdom of Fife. It sits in the park on a high place above St Margaret's Loch. We decided to go and see.

The walk took us several minutes and then we had

to climb a steep grassy escarpment to reach the chapel. We scrambled, slipping a little, as the grass was soaking wet. It would have been easy to lose one's footing and go tumbling down.

The jagged wall of the chapel stood out against the dark sky. Only the facade still stands, with a small part of one side. It was tucked into that corner that we found our father. The sight of him huddled there in the dim light brought a lump into my throat and I could see that Louisa felt similarly. To think that our father should have to live like a tramp out in the open!

He stood up to embrace us. He called us his good children. Louisa was crying now and he was stroking her back, telling her that it would be all right, everything would be sorted out soon and he would be able to come home. We did not ask how that was to come about for we suspected that he did not know himself. He seemed to think that Providence would look after him. He asked about our mother and we said that she was well and sent her love and he asked us to take good care of her. "She is not strong, you know. And she is far from her ain folk."

We stayed with him for only a few minutes as darkness was steadily encroaching on the park. Even the moon had been swallowed up by the bank of cloud. We hated having to leave him there, wrapped in a blanket, drinking soup from a can. We promised to come back the next day with more provisions and he requested that we bring him a book.

"The one lying open on my desk by the author David Hume. A philosopher, born in Edinburgh, like you children. A great man. Time moves slowly when one has nothing to read. And come in the daylight. I don't like you being abroad at night."

We kissed our father goodnight and made our way carefully back down the hill. The night seemed darker now. We passed one or two men loitering around and were relieved when we left the park behind. It is not a safe place to wander in at night. I took Louisa's arm and hurried her along. The street lamps were glowing in the town, which was a comfort. Leerie the lamplighter had been working his way around with his long pole.

As we were passing the palace gates they opened unexpectedly and a carriage and pair came swaying out. We had to jump out of the way. As it was, we got our feet spattered with mud. I just had time to glimpse two elegant-looking gentlemen sitting in the back. One might have been the Duke of Hamilton – the light was not good enough to be sure – but the other was not the Comte d'Artois. He would be as confined as my father was within the precincts, but with more comfort. When the carriage had passed we saw Monsieur Goriot coming out of the palace with another man. Their heads were bent; they were deep in conversation. We seemed to be coming across him everywhere we went, but then, I suppose it could be said that we live in a fairly small area.

We went on our way up the Canongate. Louisa kept close to me. I know she finds the closes and alleys spooky at night and I have to confess that I like to hurry past their openings myself. One never knows who will come out of the shadows.

Halfway up the Canongate, we were accosted by a drunken man who tried to seize hold of Louisa. He had just come out of Jenny Ha's Change House where sometimes our father goes, or used to go, to meet a friend and drink a glass of claret. The man wanted money. For gin, no doubt. His face was covered with sores. I dragged Louisa away and he spat on the ground behind us. His curses followed us up the street.

We were glad when we reached the warm safety of our house and Bessie awaiting us with a hot meal. Our appetites have not been good this evening, however. We cannot rid our minds of the image of our father huddling inside a ruin on one of the coldest nights of the year, at the mercy of passing footpads and other scoundrels.

Chapter 5

"I hope Dad's not sleeping rough," said Lucy, as she put the journal back in its hiding place. She was just in time, for a moment later they heard the front door opening and their mother call out, "It's only me!"

"How're you doing, Mum?" asked Will. She was looking fraught.

"I'm worried your dad might have had a nervous breakdown."

"I can't imagine it," said Will. "Not Dad."

"He's always so cheerful," said Lucy.

"It can happen to anyone when they're under a lot of stress."

Their dad must have been very stressed out, knowing that he owed all that money and had no way of repaying it. And that a man like Mr Smith was after him!

"He might have gone to see one of his friends up north," said Lucy. He had one or two buddies with whom he went hillwalking.

Their mother was not inclined to think so. In her experience, men didn't confide in each other the way women did. "Men keep things bottled up more. That's right, isn't it, Will?"

"Possibly." He made a face.

Both Lucy and her mother knew that Will did. If he arrived home from school looking down in the dumps he wouldn't tell them what was wrong, whereas Lucy would come bursting in with all her news, good and bad.

Their mother felt she had done enough phoning to people trying to pretend it was only a casual call and there was nothing wrong. She agreed to let Will phone one or two of the northern friends without telling them that Ranald had disappeared. He rang three or four numbers.

"We were just wondering if Dad might be up there?"

None of the friends had seen their father for a while.

"What about Dan?" suggested Lucy. He was one of their father's best friends.

"I did try him, a couple of times," said their mother. "But I couldn't get hold of him."

Will gave it another try and Dan answered. He said, "Ranald was supposed to call me last week and he didn't. We were going to have a game of golf. Nothing wrong, is there?"

"No, no," said Will, replacing the receiver, though he was thinking that soon, perhaps, they might have to let some people know what was going on.

"He wouldn't go to France, would he?" said Lucy, for they had relatives in France. They were not close connections, but they kept in touch with them and their father had a second or third cousin called Louis, of whom he was particularly fond. They had never been sure how far back the connection went but now Lucy herself and Will knew. They were descended from Anne-Marie, the mother of William and Louisa!

Their mother said she doubted that their dad would have gone to France though she was coming to realise that they should rule nothing out. She went upstairs to see if his passport was missing and came back with it in her hand.

"His cheque book is there too. He'd have some money in his wallet, I imagine, and his credit cards." She shook her head. "But they wouldn't be any use, would they?" For a moment she had forgotten that they had all been cancelled by the credit card companies.

The doorbell rang.

"It couldn't be that man back again!" she said.

"It could," said Lucy, squinting sideways out of the window. "I think he's alone this time."

Their mother went to the door with them following hard on her heels.

Mr Smith got his word in first. He held up his hand. "Don't say anything until you hear what I've got to say. I've got a proposition for Mr Cunningham which you might pass on to him. A way to help him out of his difficulties. We aim where possible to help people in trouble. Perhaps it would be easier if I came inside?"

A small group of American tourists in long plastic raincoats had just entered the alley, embarked on a tour of the Old Town of Edinburgh. One man was wearing a tartan tammy. "It was in closes like this," the leader was telling them, "that you might have come across the body-snatchers Burke and Hare . . ."

"Perhaps you'd better come in," said their mother, taking a step back to allow Mr Smith to pass.

They all stood about in the living room. They did not invite Mr Smith to take a seat.

"I would imagine," he began, "that we are not the only people to whom Mr Cunningham owes money?" When he received no reply he nodded and went on, "Now we could offer to consolidate all his debts into one—"

"What does that mean?" interrupted Lucy.

Her mother answered. "Put them all together so that your father would owe everything to Mr Smith's company."

"But he'd still owe the same amount," objected Will.

"That is true," agreed Mr Smith. "But we would arrange easier terms of payment than he'd get elsewhere."

"But why would you do that?"

"Yes, why would you?" added their mother. "And how could you be sure that my husband would be able to pay you back?"

"No problem." Mr Smith was wearing a broad smile now. He made Lucy think of a spider who's fairly sure he's about to get the flies trapped in his net. "We would be prepared to accept your house as collateral."

"What's that?" asked Lucy.

"He means that if we couldn't pay they would take our house in exchange," said her mother.

"But our house is worth more than fifty thousand pounds," objected Will.

"Exactly! We'll wish you good day, Mr Smith. We are not interested in your proposal."

"You might have the place sold over your heads before you're done. Forced sale. You might get peanuts for it." On his way out, he turned back to face them. "Interest is mounting every day. Tick-tock, tick-tock." He waggled his head. "Like the old grandfather clock. Tell Mr Cunningham that if you ever see him again!"

Will slammed the door behind him.

"What a horrible man!" cried Lucy. "We will see Dad again, won't we, Mum?"

"Of course!" Their mother did not sound totally confident. Her eyes were troubled. She decided to go round and talk to her friend Jane who lived nearby and was a solicitor. "Jane's usually got some sensible advice to offer."

She came back half an hour later to say Jane thought that if their father had not returned by midday tomorrow, Sunday, they should report the matter to the police. "In case he's had an accident, or a breakdown. Or something," she finished.

They had never seen their mother look so limp and that frightened them. She was usually practical and upbeat. They knew she was reluctant to go to the police for that would seem to make their father's disappearance a fact. She was still hoping, as they were, that he might walk in the door at any moment. But with each hour that passed it was seeming less likely.

"I think I'll go and lie down," she said. "I've got a bit of a headache."

Lie down? They had never heard her say that before, not in the daytime, at least.

"Let's go for a walk, Will," said Lucy.

"That's a good idea," said their mother.

Without discussing it, Lucy and Will turned their steps downhill once they reached the street. They glanced into the mouth of every close as they passed.

The alleys no longer teemed with ragged, barefoot children, and hawkers were not to be seen or heard crying their wares, as in William and Louisa's time. It was a raw day and the light was waning. There were not many people about, except for a few hardy tourists. Some came all year round but January tended to be a quiet month.

"It's January," said Lucy, struck suddenly by the coincidence. "Like it was in William and Louisa's journal. I don't suppose—"

"That would be too much of a coincidence," said Will. "It would be kind of spooky. But—"

They said no more. They broke into a run as they passed the closed gates of the Palace of Holyroodhouse and entered the park, known nowadays as the Queen's Park. Soon they were cutting across the grass and climbing up the slope towards St Anthony's Chapel.

They could see even from a little way off that there was nobody there but they pressed on anyway, until they reached the ruin.

"It would have been too much to expect," said Will, disappointed nevertheless.

"It was worth a try."

Lucy looked forlornly at the walls with their gaping holes where once there had been windows and a door. She crouched down. She had seen something interesting carved at the foot of the wall.

"Come and look, Will."

He squatted beside her. "It looks like a dagger! Another one!"

"It does, doesn't it? What's it all about?"

Will shook his head. Then his eye caught sight of a scrap of paper that someone must have dropped. He reached over and picked it up. The paper was part of a wrapper from a chocolate bar, fairly sodden, but the brand was still recognisable. It was dark chocolate, containing seventy per cent cocoa, made by a well-known Swiss firm. Their father didn't eat much chocolate. But he loved this kind. He often kept it in his pocket and when he felt his blood sugar dropping he would pop a bit into his mouth.

"He's been here," cried Lucy. "I *know* he has."

Will was inclined to agree. "Dad must have read the journal! The other Ranald Cunningham came here. And so did Dad!"

"Why has he never told us about the book?"

"Who knows? If we read on we might find out."

"I'm going to write him a note and leave it beside the wall. In case he comes back to sleep here tonight. After all, it does give some kind of shelter, doesn't it?"

Lucy had a notebook in her pocket. She wanted to be a writer when she grew up and a writer visiting her class at school had suggested keeping a notebook and jotting down ideas when they came to you.

She ripped out a page and squatting down on her hunkers she wrote their message, with Will crouching beside her.

Hi, Dad. We hope you're all right. We are. If you get this leave us a message to let us know how you're doing. We love you and miss you. Please come home.
Lucy & Will

Chapter 6

Louisa

Yesterday, Saturday, at midnight, and William and I were standing at the head of the close listening to the Tron clock strike twelve. We were excited. For twenty-four hours, almost, our father would be at home again. He would sit with us at table and eat proper food freshly prepared by Bessie. He would sleep in his own bed between newly laundered sheets instead of lying wrapped in a blanket at the mercy of the month's inclement weather.

We had wanted to go down to the Abbey Strand but our mother would not allow it. She said half the riff-raff of Edinburgh would be waiting there to welcome their criminal relatives.

"Papa is not a criminal!" William had been annoyed with her.

"I did not say that *he* was. But I am sure that some of the other debtors in Sanctuary are. Bessie tells me so. She says they are not suitable company for your dear papa. If he had any money they would rob him. My poor Ranald!" It is her constant cry these days.

"Perhaps it is as well he has no money, then," William had responded, his tongue firmly lodged in his cheek.

Within minutes of the last stroke of midnight dying away, the carriages came rattling up the hill. The air was filled with the rumble of carriage wheels, the clatter of horses' hooves on cobbles, and the cries of the drivers as they cracked their whips and urged the beasts onward and upward. Steam gushed white from the horses' nostrils into the cold night air. We could just dimly make out the noblemen who sat inside the coaches, released, like our father, from confinement for a day. They would be in a hurry to reach their destinations. Bessie, who gathered in all the news on her way up and down the street, said they would go home to sumptuous banquets awaiting them. When we asked how could they afford to have such meals she said they told the shopkeepers they would get their money later. Without a doubt, the Comte d'Artois would be taken to spend the night in one of their grand houses where he would be safe not only from debtors but from others who might wish him ill. The French monarchy has many enemies.

After the carriages came sedan chairs, and then the men on foot. Our father was to the fore of the last group. As soon as we saw him we dashed out to greet him. He hugged us both and kept his arms round our shoulders as we went down the alley to home.

Bessie was at the door. She took his hand and looked up into his face, stubbled around the chin and grown thinner even in a few days. "I'm richt pleased tae see ye, maister. Ye'll be needin' a good bath afore ye eat. I have the water bilin' fer ye." We had seen her hauling the bath of steaming water up the stairs to his bedroom. By now it would be tepid but he would not mind.

He laughed. "How right you are, Bessie!"

"And aifter that a guid hot meal."

He sniffed the air. "I smell it, Bessie! I am sure you will have cooked me a meal made from heaven."

We could do with some help from heaven to enable us to buy food. Today we were to have a stew made from a small piece of neck of mutton with potatoes and neeps. Papa would be given the best pieces of meat. We had not eaten any all week. We'd been living off porridge and bannocks for the most part and each day were not sure where our next meal would come from. But today was to be a feast day, even if our table would not be covered with platters of pork and beef, partridges and pheasants, and legs of lamb, as in the houses of the nobles.

Papa went in to greet our mother. We stood back in the lobby, listening to them murmuring and laughing together. They had not seen each other since he had run down the hill into Sanctuary. William and I had gone every day to visit him in St Anthony's Chapel but we understood that our mother did not want to go and see him there, living so wretchedly.

Bessie allowed our parents to have a little time together before she came rapping on the door saying that the water in the bath was cooling rapidly.

"Yes, you'd better go and clean yourself, Ranald." Our mother laughed. It was good to hear her laughter for she has been quite miserable of late. "You do not smell too sweet."

We had a happy meal and went late to bed, very late, for by then it was nearly morning.

We slept until midday and so missed the Sabbath morning service at St Giles. We were sad, though, that Papa had only twelve hours of freedom left.

"Twelve whole hours!" he declared. "That is a lot of time. Time has come to mean something different to me. I let each hour exist on its own and don't think about the next one."

"You might find that easy to do, Ranald," said our mother, "but we don't, do we, children?"

We would have to admit that since he has gone away the days have been dragging slowly by.

It was raining and since Papa spends much of his days in the park walking about to keep warm, he did not propose a walk now. We were pleased to stay inside with him. Bessie built the fire high in the drawing room. We played cards and then Papa and William had a game of chess while Maman did her embroidery and I played a few tunes on the pianoforte. When I turned on the stool and looked back into the room at the faces of my parents and brother looking so happy in the lamplight I could not believe that in a few more hours our peace would be shattered and Papa would be hurrying back down the hill again to his freezing ruin. But he would say not to think about that; think only about *now*.

We ate again, and the hands of the clock moved steadily round. My eyes kept straying to it. Ten o'clock. Eleven.

Bessie brought Papa some milk laced with hot brandy and a bannock and cheese.

"You'll make me fat, Bessie!"

"That'd tak' some doin'."

He had already looked out several books that he intended to take with him and put them in a sack by the door. To the bag, Bessie had added a few victuals.

"I cannot bear to think you sleep outside like beggars, Ranald!" Our mother covered her face with her hands. Her shoulders were shaking.

He went to sit beside her on the *chaise longue* and comfort her. "It will be all right soon, Anne-Marie. I am trying to work something out. And, meanwhile, I shall not be sleeping outside after tonight. I was about to tell you. I have found employment in the palace."

She removed her hands. "You have? Are you going to be a courtier to the *comte*, or his scribe?"

"No, I shall be doing something different." Papa is good at sounding vague. Especially when he has something to conceal.

"In what way?"

"Helping, generally. They need help, with so many people lodging in the palace."

"But you will work for the *comte* and his party?"

"I shall."

"That's wonderful, *chéri*! And you will be given a room to sleep in?"

"Indeed I shall. So I shall have a roof over my head by day and night."

"Can we come and visit you then?"

"No, I don't think that would be possible. They don't encourage employees to have visitors. They have to be careful about security, with French spies in the country watching the count."

"What do they want with him?"

"They're watching in case he might try to raise an army. To help his brother Louis lay claim to the French throne."

Our mother nodded. "I understand that. So, from tomorrow you have a bed in the palace?"

"Papa," said William, "you must watch your time."

The hands of the wall clock stood at twenty minutes before twelve. Our parents made their farewells and then William and I walked Papa up to the street. The carriages were back again, this time rolling in the opposite direction, downward.

"Can we come and see you tomorrow?" I asked.

"I shall try to come outside some time in the late afternoon but I cannot promise. My duties may prevent it. You might come after you finish your studies and see if I'm there. You must keep them up until my return." Normally, he taught us. But these not being normal times, we would have to study by ourselves.

Then I noticed the man. The messenger-at-arms with his ebony stick. He was waiting on the other side of the road.

"Look, Papa!" I cried.

"You'd better go!" urged William.

We quickly kissed him goodbye. As he moved off we saw that the messenger did too.

Papa was walking fast, going well ahead of his pursuer. With the going being downhill he should make it over the line, but with only a few minutes to spare. While we stood there another man with an ebony stick passed by in pursuit of his quarry.

"Do you think Papa really has a job in the palace?" asked William.

"Papa never lies."

"That is true. So, in that case, he must have one."

We resolved to go down to the palace the next day and look for him.

Maman was in a cheerful mood when we went back to her. "Is it not *merveilleuse* that your father is working for the Comte d'Artois? The *Comte*! Perhaps we shall now be able to buy some better meat."

"Maman," said William, "remember that the *comte* is living in the palace because he has no money. He owes millions of francs. I don't know how much he'll be able to pay Papa."

"Ah, but Bessie tells me that the British government is to give him six thousand pounds a year for his living expenses."

"Six thousand pounds," we echoed.

"Why would our government give all that money to a citizen of *France*?" asked William.

"I do not like the tone of your voice, William. Let me remind you that I have come from France."

"They don't give you money."

"They wouldn't give any to Papa either, would they?" I put in. "And he pays taxes here." Or he did, when he could.

"But, child, the *Comte* is a nobleman and brother of a

former king of France, and possibly of the next king. He could not be allowed to starve."

We let the subject drop because we know our mother is a great admirer of the French royal family. She'd been distraught when she'd heard of the execution of the king and queen; not that we were indifferent to it ourselves.

I am left thinking that if what Bessie says is true about the six thousand pounds then perhaps our father will earn enough money to pay off his debts. And then he would be able to come home.

I am about to go to bed, feeling more cheerful than I have since he entered Sanctuary.

Chapter 7

It was half past eleven on Sunday morning. They had been watching the clock since they'd got up. Only half an hour was left for their father to turn up before they went to report him missing. They wouldn't have far to go; the police station was just down the road. Their mother had gone out to a café to have coffee with Jane.

"Pity we don't have Sanctuary now," said Lucy. "At least William and Louisa knew where their dad was." As their mother kept saying, it was the not knowing that made it all so difficult. And William and Louisa had been able to spend Sundays with their dad. This was promising to be a very slow Sunday.

At midday their mother returned, with Jane.

"When you talk to the police don't start straight in about your dad's debts in case they jump to conclusions," advised Jane. "After all, that might not be the reason he's gone. It's important to keep an open mind."

But Will and Lucy, thinking of the other Ranald Cunningham, felt convinced that it was.

"Take a photograph with you," added Jane.

They rummaged amongst the photos in the various shoeboxes which they kept meaning to sort out one day but somehow never got round to. They found a good clear likeness of their dad standing on the beach at North Berwick holding a ball above his head, ready to throw to someone. One of them. They didn't have a plain head-and-shoulders photograph, apart from his passport one, which made him look like a thug. That was the last thing they wanted to take along to the police station. On the beach he looked handsome, and he was smiling.

Jane walked with them as far as the police station entrance and then left them, after warning them not to expect too much. "I doubt if they'll have any information to give you."

After they'd told the sergeant on the desk why they'd come, a friendly policewoman took them into a small stuffy room and seated them round a table. Their mother passed over the photograph.

"Looks like he didn't have a care in the world there," observed the constable.

"That was last summer," said Lucy, remembering the bright sunny day and the fun they'd had playing ball. Afterwards they'd gone up the street to the chipper to buy fish and chips and come back to walk on the sand and eat them.

After the constable had written down all the basic details – the missing person's name, age, address, profession, height, build, colouring – she asked each of them when they had last seen him. When she heard it was only two days ago she appeared to take their case less seriously.

"He might have had a weekend out with the boys and not been able to make it home. It's been known."

"That wouldn't be like him," said their mother. "He goes to the pub for an hour or two occasionally but he's not much of a drinker."

The policewoman shrugged. "We can all act out of character at times."

Their mother had to admit that was true. Wherever their father had gone, or whatever he'd done, it was not in his character, as they knew it.

"What was he wearing on Thursday morning when you last saw him?"

"Light fawn trousers, pale blue shirt – yes, I'm sure that's what he had on – and a dark blue jacket."

"No tie?"

"No."

"Any distinguishing marks?"

It was mention of the latter that made Lucy begin to feel sick. She realised that they needed to know about distinguishing marks in case they found a body.

"Not really," said their mother. "He did have a small scar on his forehead from when he fell off a bike when he was a kid." She broke off, looking at Lucy. "Are you feeling all right, love?"

"Why don't you go out and get some air, dear?" suggested the policewoman.

Lucy went out into the street and threw up in the gutter.

Meanwhile, back in the airless room, the constable was asking Will and his mother if they had any idea why Mr Cunningham might leave home voluntarily. "I'm presuming you don't think he's been taken against his will?"

"Of course not," answered his wife hurriedly.

"He didn't ever deal in anything illegal?"

She means drugs, thought Will indignantly. Maybe she thinks he's been involved in a drug war and been made to disappear. "He would never do that," he said.

"What about any other attachments?"

"If you mean another woman in his life," said Will's mother, two red spots burning brightly high up on her cheeks, "the answer is no."

"You can be absolutely sure of that?"

"Yes," said Will sharply.

"Let your mother answer for herself, son."

"I'm pretty certain."

"Pretty certain," the policewoman was writing down.

She doesn't believe half we're telling her, thought Will.

"Why are you pretty certain, Mrs Cunningham? Men don't always tell us wives what they're up to."

"Because we know why he's gone. At least we *think* we do."

"You do? I see." The constable sat back.

"He was in debt."

"Ah . . . Heavily?"

"Yes."

"Can you tell me everything you know?"

When they had told everything the policewoman said she'd heard this story only too often before.

"They start by running up a credit card or a store card until it's blocked, then they open another and begin all over again. It's the slippery slope. It only leads downward, into a nightmare."

Will felt his heart take a downward slide. He felt as if they were in the bottom of a pit without footholds to climb up by. How could their father ever get the money together to pay off his debts? How could *they*?

"Does he have a car?"

"No. We sold it six months ago, to economise. We don't really need one, living in the centre of Edinburgh."

"That was wise, at any rate. Not much else that he did seemed to be. I bet he was buying lottery tickets?"

Will remembered his dad checking the numbers online one day and had been surprised. He used to be dead against the lottery, saying it was a fool's way to lose money.

The policewoman said they'd check the hospitals but they'd had no reports of any unidentified men being brought in over the weekend. They would put his details on file and keep an eye out for him, but they couldn't promise much. People went missing by the thousand every year.

"Mostly because they want to. They scarper when there's trouble and start up a different life elsewhere. Or try to."

"Our father's not like that," said Will.

"That's good then, son. And listen, don't give up hope. It's only been two days. My bet is that he'll turn up before long. He sounds like a good guy, just no good with money."

"He *is* a good guy!"

"Let us know if he does turn up."

They went outside to find Lucy leaning against the wall. She didn't see them for a moment and jumped when she did.

"Try not to worry too much, love," said her mother.

"You're worrying though, aren't you?"

"The policewoman says he'll probably just turn up."

"What does she know?"

"Coming for a walk, Luce?" said Will.

"Here!" Their mother took some money from her purse and gave it to Will. "Go and have a Coke or a hot chocolate or something." She normally wouldn't give them money to buy Coke. She thought it was bad for them.

They parted and Will and Lucy went to a nearby café where they had hot chocolate. It was such a cold day they needed warming up.

"I hope Dad's not wandering about in this weather," said Lucy, cradling her mug with both hands. Temperatures had been right down to zero in the last few days. "Shall we go and see if he's been back to the chapel?"

They finished their drinks and carried on down the hill, past the palace, round Horse Wynd and into the park. A jogger puffed by, his breathing harsh, his breath white in the chill air. The grass was frozen. The stalks felt stiff under their feet.

The ruin of St Anthony's Chapel was as abandoned as it had been on their previous visit. Lucy went at once to the place in the wall where she had left their note. It was still there.

"He can't have been here."

"Pick it up," said Will. "Let's have a look. In case he's left us a message."

But he had not. There were the words that Lucy had written, a little blurred by damp, but nothing more. The slender link that they'd hoped they might have had with their father had snapped.

Chapter 8

William

As soon as we had finished lunch – a hunk of bread with gravy left from yesterday's stew – Louisa and I rose from the table and went to fetch our coats. We had worked hard at Latin and mathematics in the morning so our mother had said we could go. I think, too, she was eager for us to find out what work our father was doing for the *comte*.

"I expect he has been given employment because he speak French. His accent is very good for a Scotchman. The *comte* will have realised that your father is a man of learning. Unlike some of our neighbours!"

She does not care in particular for Mrs Alexander who keeps the Rook Tavern. Maman says the inn brings undesirable people into the close. One cannot deny that drunk men can be a nuisance. They are noisy and they urinate on the steps. Previously lawyers used to reside here and in other closes nearby but they have been moving out to go and live down in the New Town, which has wide, open streets, and the houses are only three or four storeys high. This is where Maman herself would like to live. Our father says he was born in this house, and here he will die.

"There is less stink down in the New Town," says our mother.

It is true that the streets in the Old Town smell badly, especially in the late evening when people shout "Gardy loo!" and empty the contents of their chamber pots out of the window. One has to make haste to get out of the way. The ordure then lies in the gutters until seven in the morning when the scavengers come with their wheelbarrows to clean it up. It is jokingly known as "the flowers of Edinburgh"! Maman is not amused. She is indignant, also, that people cannot even pronounce "Gardy loo!" correctly. It is a French phrase and should be "*Gardez l'eau!*" Mind the water!

Not everyone in the street throws their waste out of the window, though. We do not. Bessie carries ours up to the street late at night when most people are abed. When our mother complains about the procedure our father retaliates by saying that some French toilet habits are no more hygienic.

If the smells are very bad we burn sheets of brown paper to neutralize them. And when we go out Maman insists on giving us little bundles of French lavender wrapped in muslin to hold in front of our noses. Louisa uses hers. I certainly do not – I hold my nose if the stench is overpowering.

Maman gave us each a lavender pouch now. Louisa put on her cloak which has a hood attached. Bessie fussed over my uncovered head and insisted on winding a woollen scarf twice around my neck, which I would unwind as soon as I reached the street. I hate anything tight at my neck. There had been a light fall of snow in the night. We were glad to think that our father would sleep tonight within the shelter of the palace.

Bessie gave me a parcel of bread and cheese to take to him.

"He won't need that now, Bessie," said our mother. "He will be fed well in the palace."

"Best tae mak' sicher."

Bessie always likes to make sure.

A few white flakes were drifting out of the heavy sky as we made our way down the hill. The street was more slippery than usual so we went carefully. There is always so much refuse lying around that one's clothes get soiled if one falls. And of course we have fallen from time to time when running or playing tag. We have to do that out of sight of our mother!

Barefooted children were still out playing in spite of the cold day, scooping up snow and trying to make it into balls, even though no more than a skim lay on the ground. A boy tried to throw one at us but it fell apart in mid-flight.

There were still traders about in the High Street, though the Abbey Strand was virtually deserted, apart from a couple of caddies hanging around outside the taverns hoping a 'laird' might appear and give them a message to deliver. The sootyman came into sight with his brushes and bag of soot on his back, leaving a little trail of black behind him in the white snow. He gave us a wave as he headed up the hill. He had cleaned our chimneys only the week before.

There was no sign of our father at the palace. There was nothing we could do but loiter around the side gate and hope he might come out at some point.

An old woman in a ragged shawl came to speak to us. She eyed my parcel.

"Have ye ony food? I'm stairvin.'"

"It's for our father," said Louisa.

The woman looked at our clothes. "He'll nae be stairvin'. Thon's fine coats ye're wearin.'" She stretched out a hand and fingered the cloth of Louisa's cape. "Braw. Ye can spare a bite fer a puir oul wuman, surely?"

I broke off a piece of bread in the bag and gave it to her. I thought that what our mother had said would make sense. If Papa were employed in the palace he would be fed. But was he? The doubt still lingered and made me feel guilty that I should think my father capable of lying.

A carriage swirled past us and inside we made out a woman and a boy of perhaps eleven or twelve years old.

"Thon's the count's lady friend, Madame de Polastron," said our companion. "And her son, Louis. They say he's the count's son!"

"How do you know?" asked Louisa.

"I hear a' the gossip in the tavern." She told us that the Polastrons were living in a whitewashed house on the left of the chapel, at the entrance of Croft-an-Righ.

For a while nothing else happened. The snow thickened and now I was glad of the scarf Bessie had pressed on me. The woman in the shawl left us and we watched her go into one of the taverns; to beg a drink from somebody, we presumed. Our feet felt like ice blocks even though we stamped them hard and walked up and down. We were beginning to think we would have to go home when we saw a man coming towards the gate from within the palace grounds. He was on foot, and not grandly dressed, so we thought we could accost him. He looked as if he might be employed in the palace himself.

"Excuse me, sir," I began.

He stopped and asked if he could be of any help. He seemed a genial fellow.

"We're waiting for our father," said Louisa. "He's employed in the palace."

"What's his name?"

We told him and he frowned. "Don't know him but then there's dozens workin' about the place, especially since the Frenchies came."

"He just started today," I said.

"What kind of work will he be doin'?"

"We're not sure. He didn't say."

"He's a scholar," put in Louisa. "And he can write in French."

"He might be a clerk to the count then."

"He said he'd try to come out to see us but we don't know how long to wait."

"If ye hang on a wee while ye can come back in wi' me. But first I've got an errand to do."

"Would it be all right for us to come in?" I asked.

"Nae bother. There's so many folk living in the palace, what wi' the Frenchies and our own noblemen and their wives and children and servants, that nobody would notice ye."

He told us to call him Tam and we walked with him up to Halkerstoun's Wynd. He had come to place an order at Mr Charles the candlemaker's for several dozen candles. He said he would take a box with him now and perhaps we, too, could each carry one? We readily agreed, for that would make us feel less conspicuous going into the palace. The remaining candles were to be delivered.

"And when am I to get my money?" demanded Mr Charles.

Tam shrugged. "That's nae up to me. Ye can send yer bill."

"I'm already owed plenty."

In spite of that, grumbling somewhat, he gave Tam the candles.

The door opened behind us and I glanced round briefly to see who had come in. It was Monsieur Goriot.

Mr Charles was looking at Louisa and myself and frowning. "Are you not Ranald Cunningham's children?"

"We are," said Louisa, lifting her chin. I was feeling uneasy.

"He owes me money and all. Half the folk in Edinburgh do." I wondered if that would apply to Monsieur Goriot too. We were about to leave when Mr Charles said, "Wait a minute till I get you his bill. I've already sent him one but he has neglected to pay."

"I'm sorry," said Louisa.

I kept silent. I dreaded to think in how many shops around the town we might be similarly greeted.

The candlemaker searched in a drawer and produced the bill. He put it into my hand. "Tell him I would appreciate an early settlement."

I hoped that we would have a good supply of candles in the house for we would not be able to come back here to order more. At that moment I felt annoyed with my father that he should have been so bad at looking after his affairs. After all, I thought, the candlemaker also has to eat, and feed his children. As we passed Monsieur Goriot I stared hard at him wondering how many crowns Papa had actually 'lent' him. He stared back at me. I knew there would be no chance of him offering to repay any of Papa's money. I left the shop with a jumble of feelings turning inside me.

We trudged behind Tam in blinding snow back to the palace. I could see only the shape of his back through the whirl of white. His footprints faded as fast as he left them. I looked back at Louisa. The boxes were heavy and I was worried that it might be too much for her but she seemed to be managing even though her feet were slipping.

We went through the gates and entered the palace by a rear door. The guard nodded, recognising Tam, and paid no attention to us. I could not help thinking that spies from France or elsewhere would find it fairly easy to gain access.

It was obvious that we were in the servants' quarters. The passage was dingy and cold. We passed several servants, both male and female, going about their business, some of the latter carrying mops and pails. I supposed it would take a huge number of people to look after a place as big as this.

Tam led us through a doorway into a storeroom where we deposited the boxes of candles. Two men were working there, sorting out sacks and boxes. Tam asked if they had come across a Ranald Cunningham working in the palace. They shook their heads.

"I'm busy the now so just tak' a wee dander round yersel's," said Tam. "Ye might run into him."

We thanked him and a little apprehensively did as he had suggested. But there were so many people around that perhaps we would not be noticed. We thought that our father, if he were employed as a clerk, would not be in the servants' quarters, but in the main part of the palace. We found a door which, when we pushed it open, led us into a hall. It looked rather scruffy but it had gilt-framed pictures on the walls. As we stood wondering what to do, two men wearing wigs and well-cut coats and knee breeches came along chatting to each other. In French.

"*Bonjour*," said one, as they passed us.

"*Bonjour*," we chorused in return.

It seemed like a safe password to use.

We proceeded along the corridor, lit by flares on the walls. We glanced into rooms where the doors stood open and saw that everything was in a somewhat run-down state. Hangings were tattered and faded, carpets had holes in them, and the brocade chairs with the gilt legs looked in need of a clean. How Bessie would love to get her hands on them! It did not seem a very grand place for a royal nobleman, brother of the former king of France. But better than a gaol.

We met several other men in varying kinds of dress,

some elegant and bewigged, others more ordinary, marking them out as servants. When anyone gave us a curious look we said, "*Bonjour*". After we had said it three times, Louisa giggled. "They'll think we're part of the *comte*'s family."

There was still no sign of our father.

"He might be behind one of the closed doors," said Louisa.

"We can't open any of those."

"We won't find out unless we look."

"But we don't know who might be in there. Even the *comte* himself."

"I shall just say, '*Pardon!*' very politely."

And with that, Louisa, who is impetuous, opened the door and put her head inside. Then she said, "*Pardon!*" and closed it hurriedly.

"A sitting room," she whispered. "Lots of people."

The door opened again and out came a butler carrying an empty silver tray. He was rather grandly dressed for a servant, with flounces and silver-buckled shoes. Perhaps he was the head butler. He gave us a superior look.

"*Bonjour*," we said, but he responded in English.

"Whit do the twa of ye want snoopin' aboot in here? Ye dinne belong here, do ye? I've no seen ye afore."

"We're looking for our father," I said.

"He is employed by the count," added Louisa, tossing her head, annoyed, I could see, by the man's disdainful air.

"Is that so?"

"His name is Ranald Cunningham," I said.

"Niver heard of him," said the man and he began to hustle us along the corridor, whilst keeping the silver tray balanced aloft on the palm of one hand. I could not help wishing that he would trip and the tray go shooting off into space. "I suggest ye ask doon the stairs where the skivvies work."

He stopped at the door we had entered the corridor by previously, pushed it open and held it there until we had passed through, then he let it swing shut behind us. It struck me on the back.

"I am glad Papa is not working for him!" declared Louisa.

We wandered back along the corridor and into another one. What the man had said about skivvies lay uneasily on my mind though I said nothing to Louisa. We were approaching the kitchens. We could smell cooking and hear the clatter of pots. The door of the first room we came to was ajar. We stopped and looked in.

The light was bleak but we could make out two men in long canvas aprons standing in front of two big stone sinks, washing pots and pans. One of them was our father.

We turned immediately and walked swiftly back along the corridor and out into the winter afternoon. We knew that our father would not have wished us to see him.

As we were passing Jenny Ha's tavern the door opened

and out came a man whom I recognised, even in that poor light. He was the man who had accompanied our messenger-at-arms. He had a slanty eye, which was unmistakable. He recognised us, too.

"Been to see yer da, have ye? We'll get him yet. He'll nae escape us. Tell him that fer me, will ye?"

Chapter 9

In school, on Monday afternoon, the day after they had been to the police station to report their father missing, Lucy found it difficult to concentrate on French, which normally she enjoyed. They went most summers to France on holiday though it wasn't likely they'd be going this year. Not unless a miracle happened. She couldn't help thinking about her dad; the fact that he was MISSING. Sometimes you read about cases like that in the paper or saw it on TV, though usually a girl was involved if it was on the telly. Last seen . . . You never imagined it could happen to anyone in your family.

When she wasn't thinking about her father she was thinking about William and Louisa's. They might have been upset at seeing him washing dishes in the palace but that was better than not seeing him at all. She and Will didn't have a clue where their father was or what he was doing. Not a single clue.

On her way out of the classroom at the end of the afternoon, the teacher stopped her and asked if there was anything wrong. "Something worrying you, Lucy?"

She shook her head. How could she possibly tell Miss Harper? She couldn't even tell Julie, her best friend. Julie kept chattering all the way down the road, about a top she had seen in a shop and hoped her mum was going to buy for her, and she didn't even seem to notice that Lucy was saying nothing. Sometimes Lucy got fed up hearing about Julie's new clothes. Her own mum couldn't afford to buy her as much. And with all these debts round their ears She'd be able to afford even less in future, if anything.

When she and Julie came to the parting of their ways, they stopped on the corner to blether as they always did. Sometimes they'd stand for as long as half an hour, or even an hour.

Today Lucy said, "There's Will." She'd caught sight of him on the other side of the road. He was alone, not with his friend Mark, as he usually was. "I'll chum him home."

Julie looked surprised but only said, "OK then. See you tomorrow. I might ring you later."

Lucy dashed across the road during a break in the traffic and as she did so she thought that her father would have been annoyed if he could have seen her. He always told them to cross at the lights. She just couldn't get him out of her head, not even for a minute, it seemed.

Will didn't notice she was coming until she was almost on top of him. He had been walking with his head down.

"Hi!"

That was all they said on the road home.

Their mother would still be at work, though she should be back at six tonight. Will opened the door and Lucy picked up the mail lying at the back of the door.

"Anything interesting?" Will peered over her shoulder.

"Bills," she muttered. Bills, bills and more bills. And letters from credit card companies. Apart from those, there was some junk mail.

They went into the living room and flung their bags on the floor. When their mother came in she would give them a row. *How many times do I have to tell you . . .?*

As Lucy put the mail down on the table she saw a postcard lying there. It was a picture of Holyrood Palace. She lifted it up. "Who's this from?" She turned it over. *"Dad!"* She had to sit down.

"Let me see!" Will took hold of the other edge of the card.

The writing was shaky and almost illegible.

So sorry. Need time. I love you all. Ronald.

"I wonder when he posted that?" said Lucy.

"But he didn't post it, did he? There's no postmark on it. And it was lying on the table."

"How could it get here?"

"There's only one way, isn't there?"

"Dad's been in?" said Lucy slowly.

"He must have been. He'll have his key."

"He couldn't still *be* here, could he?"

They tore up the stairs and went through every room and cupboard but there was no sign of him.

"Now we know he's alive," said Lucy.

"Were you thinking he wasn't?"

She shrugged.

They felt more cheerful now, though, and realised they were hungry. They went back downstairs and made grilled cheese on toast and hot chocolate. Neither had eaten much at lunchtime. Afterwards, Will went up to his room to do his homework and Lucy settled at the kitchen table to do hers.

She had only written one sentence when her mobile rang. She pounced on it.

"My mum got me the top," said Julie. "She'd said she wasn't going to, she says I have enough tops, but when she saw it she thought it was kind of cute."

Julie rattled on and Lucy made a face at the wall. Eventually she said, "I must go and get on with my French."

"Swot!" said Julie. "See you later!"

Lucy had just clicked her mobile off when the landline telephone rang. She seized the receiver. The recorded voice of a man came on. It was a very smooth voice.

"Congratulations! I am calling to tell you that you have been selected for today's prize draw." Lucy made another face at the wall and was about to put the phone down when she decided to listen. "You are guaranteed to have won one of the following prizes. One thousand pounds in cash. A five-thousand-pound holiday voucher. A BMW. There are no catches. The draw is valid only for today. You must phone the following number . . ." Lucy quickly seized a pen and scribbled the number on the back of her French jotter. The call terminated.

She sat back. The hand that had been gripping the receiver was sweating. The voice had said they were *guaranteed* to win one of the prizes. Any of those amounts of money would help, even the thousand. Even! They were desperate for any amount of money.

And he'd said there were no catches. If there were only three prizes and you were guaranteed to win one then he must be ringing only three people. It wouldn't make sense for him to ring more since if everyone took up the offer they wouldn't have enough prizes to go round. It was worth a call, surely? Just to find out.

Her fingers still damp, she dialled the number. She got another recorded voice. She was listening intently to the next set of instructions when the door opened at her back and Will came in. She covered the receiver with her hand.

"Who are you talking to? Julie?"

"No. Nobody."

"Must be talking to somebody. What are you up to?"

"None of your business." Lucy put the receiver down and turned her jotter over so that he wouldn't see the number. He turned it back and she grabbed it – but not before he'd seen the first four digits.

"0906. Not talking to a call centre, are you? Calls to that number cost something like sixty pence a minute."

"All right, nosyboots, I'll tell you! We have just won a prize in a draw – no, *wait*! It is *guaranteed*."

"Who says?"

"The man who rang. One of the prizes is a car. We could sell it. Pay off some of Dad's debts."

Will groaned. "Don't tell me you fell for it."

"What have we got to lose trying?"

"Sixty pence a minute on the phone line. And they'll keep you on as long as possible giving you other numbers to call. That's how they make their money. Thousands will phone in. And in the end there will be a catch. They're not giving anything away for nothing. Why should they?"

"How do you know?"

Will was looking a bit sheepish. "I tried it myself one day. I was hoping to get a stereo for my room."

Lucy burst out laughing and he joined in.

They were laughing when they heard their mother's key in the lock. The first thing she saw opening the living-room door were the bags on the floor but as soon as she opened her mouth to say her usual piece, Lucy cut across her.

"Mum, Dad's been in."

"*What?*"

She, too, had to sit down to read the card. She spoke the words aloud in a slow, puzzled voice and said, "Poor Ranald. Look at his writing. He must be in a very disturbed state. He needs help, that's obvious." She shook her head. "I wish he'd stayed till we came in. Has he been in any of the other rooms, do you know?"

"Not that we could tell," said Will.

Their mother went to look for herself. They followed

her up the stairs into the bedroom. She opened the wardrobe door and trawled along the rail. "A pair of jeans are missing. His new ones. They were there this morning."

She looked in all the cupboards and drawers. "I'm pretty sure he's taken a sweatshirt – the blue and grey one – and his black sweater and some socks and underwear." She opened another door. "And his trainers. And his sports bag isn't here." She sat back on her heels. "It looks like he was planning to go away somewhere."

"He might have gone to Orkney," suggested Lucy.

"Why would he?"

"He always says he feels away from it all when he's there."

"He might have gone anywhere," said Will.

They went back downstairs.

The phone rang in the middle of their meal. It often did. This was the time of day when people knew they could catch you at home. Lucy, who was nearly always first at the receiver, answered it.

"Tell them we're eating," said her mother. "And if they're selling anything don't waste your breath."

"It's Gran." Lucy held out the receiver.

Her mother took it. "We're all fine, thanks, Mum. Yes, the children are well. I've been meaning to ring you. No, I know we've not seen you . . . Sunday? Yes,

I think we're free Sunday." She glanced over at the children. They looked blank. "Come for lunch. See you then."

"I'll have to tell her," she said, when she had sat down again.

"You never know," said Lucy, "Dad might be home by Sunday."

"Somehow," said her mother, "I very much doubt it."

Chapter 10

Louisa

We have not managed to see Papa at all during the week even though we have gone down every day and hung around the Abbey Strand. We saw Tam on one occasion and he stopped to speak to us.

"Did ye find yer faither?"

William nodded.

"He's working as a skivvy in the scullery washing dishes," I burst out and William gave me a look. I knew he would not have told Tam but I could not help myself. I kept seeing the image of my father bent over the sink. He'd looked as if he had shrunk.

"It's hard work, that," said Tam.

"Where will he sleep, do you know?" I asked.

"I'm nae sure. He'll likely just doss doon on the flair."

"In the *scullery*?"

"Aye."

"But the floor's hard and cold!"

"So is the ground," said William quietly and I subsided.

Tam wished us goodbye and went about his business.

We also came across the old woman in the shawl or, rather, she came across us. She latched on every time she saw us but she knew all the gossip and so we did not mind. It helped to pass the time while we waited. Her name was Peg.

"Ye're wastin' yer time," she told us. "Yer faither'll nae come oot in this cold, nae aifter he's been workin' a' day. They're only fit tae drop when they finish, they skivvies."

Whenever any nobles went past she told us who they were. "There gaes the Duke of Buccleuch . . . He always looks right stuck up. And yon's Lord Dalkeith..." People went in and out all day: visitors, servants, workmen. Peg said that they were fixing up the royal apartments, to make them fit for a king.

The names of the French courtiers were too difficult for her but she said she could tell when someone was a Frenchie. She said you knew by the way they swaggered. "See that one!" She pointed a filthy finger at a man who was standing on the other side of the road with his back to us. "He's one of the count's men but he's up to nae guid, if ye ask me."

He looked round as if he had heard her though I did not think that he could have done. Peg's voice is hoarse from the smoking of a clay pipe and would scarcely carry that far. Also, there was much traffic about, with coachmen cracking their whips and carters shouting to each other.

We recognised the man. He had grown familiar to us.

"It's Monsieur Goriot," I said.

"Ye ken him then?"

"Only to see in the street. We have never spoken."

He was coming across the road. As he went past Peg, his long nose lifted in a sneer. You often see nobles putting on that kind of face when they encounter what they call 'the lower orders'. Our father says that no one has the right to look down on others. One's rank in life depends so much on good fortune. He quotes our poet Robert Burns: "A man's a man for a' that."

The Frenchman crossed the road and, after pausing to glance around, went through the main palace gates.

"So you think he's up to no good?" I said, to prompt Peg. I was prepared to believe that what she said was true.

She lowered her voice, unnecessarily now, and leaned in to us. She does smell very badly. She said, "He's up tae somethin'. I saw him in the howff las' night" – that's what Peg calls a tavern –"and I overheard him talkin' wi' anither man."

"But he's French, isn't he?"

"Nae doot."

"So how could you understand what he was saying?" It was not possible that Peg could speak French!

"I didne need tae unnerstan'. I could tell by the way they spake. Secretive like. In whispers. Lookin' aroun' tae see if onybody was listenin'."

"And you were, Peg!"

"They wudne bother aboot me. But there's nae fleas on Oul' Peg!"

I thought that there well might be so I moved back a bit. Our mother is furious when we bring in fleas. She tells us to keep away from the other children in the street but at times we do go and play tag with them, and William has been known to get into one of the bickers on a Saturday afternoon. He does not set out to fight but at times he gets drawn in. Maman does not know about the bickers, when boys coming from different parts of the town meet up. They start bickering and pelt each other with stones. Sometimes the Town Guard breaks it up but if they do the boys unite against them.

William got into a fight that day on the way back home. As we were coming past the Tron Kirk a couple of boys began to follow and taunt us about our father. We know them; they live near us. It is no secret that our father is in Sanctuary. How could it be? The boys shouted insults, calling Papa a crook and a thief.

"He is not!" I shouted back at them.

William, who is slow to boil up compared with me, eventually turned to confront them, unable to stand any more. "Take all that back!" he yelled.

"What are ye goin' tae do aboot it?"

"Come on, William." I tried to take hold of his arm but he shook me off.

He was on fire. He went forward to meet them, his fists up. He was broader and taller than they were but they lashed out with their feet and the bigger of the two had a stone in his hand. I saw his arm go up in an arc. I screamed but William had no time to dodge. The stone struck him a glancing blow on the cheek, enraging him further. He retaliated by swinging his fist and landing a powerful punch straight in the middle of the boy's face. The boy went down, blood spouting from his nose. His friend hesitated, then turned and ran. William helped up the fallen boy who, after he'd run off a few yards, cried back, "We'll get ye next time."

With a posse of reinforcements, no doubt. The incident troubled me more than it might have done ordinarily. I felt as if half of Edinburgh was out to get us or our father.

When we reached home, William's cheek was the first thing our mother noticed.

"Have you been in a fight, William?"

"Boys are aye fightin'," put in Bessie.

"William is forbidden to. It is only the riff-raff who fight. Oh, how I wish we could move to the New Town."

Little does Maman know that, sometimes, on a Saturday, a group of New Town boys come up to do battle with the boys of the Old Town, who then all join up together.

A row ensued, but William did not reveal why he had been in the fight and by the time our father came home on Saturday midnight the mark had all but faded.

Papa looked weary on this second visit, very weary. And he had a hacking cough. We saw a big change in him in that one week.

"They must be working you too hard," said our mother. "I did not think the *comte* would be a slave-driver. Have you told him that you are married to one of his countrywomen?"

"I have not had the opportunity, Anne-Marie."

"Then you must when you have it. And are you eating enough? You look thin. Is the palace food so poor?"

Our father coped well with all our mother's questions and she gave them a rest for the remainder of the twenty-four hours. He went to bed and slept for fully twelve of them and even then had to be wakened.

Too soon, Sunday evening came round again.

Bessie had made up a parcel of food, as she had done the week before.

"He shouldn't need that, Bessie," said our mother, coming into the kitchen. I was there already and had been helping Bessie to put it together. "We're short enough of food ourselves, heaven knows. They are bound to have good food in the palace. Didn't you say that the fleshers and bakers were doing good trade with the French court?"

"I doot they're gettin' paid."

"That's beside the point. They're supplying the food. And knowing my French compatriots, they will insist for it to be well cooked. The beef will not be scorched to death."

"Let Papa have it, Maman," I pleaded. "I feel sure he needs it."

"I will ask him if he does."

"He'll say no," I cried.

But she had already left the kitchen. She came back a few minutes later to say that Papa insisted we keep all the food for ourselves. "He says you children grow all the time like shoots and need much food to make strong bones."

When she had gone again I said, "Bessie, I *know* he needs it. I can't tell you how we know – William and I – but you can take my word for it that we do. Look how thin he is!"

"Dinne fash yersel'. Ye'll be walkin' him oot tae the street? When ye go oot the door I'll slip ye this parcel. Ye can put it under yer cloak and gie it tae him when he leaves the close."

She added that maybe she should not be doing this behind my mother's back but the health of the master was more important. She had known him since he was a boy and had worked for his mother and father in this same house.

And so we did as she had suggested. I held the package snugly under my cloak all the way up the close. At the top, our father turned to wave goodbye to our mother and Bessie, then we turned into the street.

Before I had the chance to pass over the parcel, I saw the messenger-at-arms with his slanty-eyed companion. He was standing across the street waiting for Papa. William and I placed ourselves on either side of him.

"Papa," said William, "let us walk with you as far as the sanctuary tonight. No harm will come to us on the way home. The street is full of people and the Town Guard are about."

"There is no need for you to do that. You should be in your beds."

"Papa," I said, "the messenger-at-arms is over there. He has the Wand of Peace with him."

"*Papa*," said William urgently, taking hold of his arm, "we *insist*."

I took his other arm and we set off, our father still complaining, though only mildly. He had stopped once he saw that, indeed, we were being followed. Like the weekend before, he had left his departure a little late, lingering over his farewells with our mother, so we had to walk fast. We kept to the middle of the street as much as possible since the gutters are even worse on a Sunday night, with the scaffies not working on the Sabbath. Every now and then, however, we had to duck into the side to allow carriages and sedan chairs to sail past. Not that the sedans sail so smoothly. They lurch considerably on the rough road and their occupants are tossed from side to side.

I glanced up at the Tron clock. Nine minutes to go.

I noticed that our follower and his friend had moved ahead, though they kept turning back to check on us. We passed the Netherbow and the Canongate church and could now see the bottom of the hill. Some people were running but I did not think our father was fit enough for that. I resolved that next Sunday we would force him to leave earlier.

"Hurry, Papa, hurry!" urged Will.

He was doing his best. Once he skidded and would have fallen had we not held on to him. "Five minutes," said somebody behind us. We broke into a jogging-trot. By now we were in the middle of a large crowd. When we reached the foot of the Canongate we all surged across the road together, rounding the Girth Cross, making for the Abbey Strand, which lay but a few yards away, and for safety.

Waiting close to the sanctuary boundary was a number of people, amongst them our two enemies. They had their eyes fixed on us. I thought we should be able to get past them in time but with no more than a minute to spare.

And then, too late, I saw the warrant officer nod at a

man in a grey coat standing on the opposite side of the street. At that instant we drew level and the man in grey stuck out his foot and, hooking it around William's leg, brought him down. Our father was thus tilted sideways. He staggered and fell right across the boundary line where he lay, winded, his head and shoulders in Sanctuary, the rest of him not.

Quickly William scrambled up and between us we seized our father by the shoulders and began to drag him. The men descended on us, shouting that it was midnight – we could hear the chimes – and our father was theirs! The messenger-at-arms was trying to strike our father with his ebony wand whilst the others endeavoured to push us out of the way, but we hung on. We managed to clear Papa's feet from the boundary, but only just. We sat down on the road beside him, panting. He was looking dazed. I heard a cheer and looking up saw Peg waving to us. The men we'd outwitted were cursing us soundly.

After we had got our breath back we were able to rise and brush ourselves down a little. Bessie would have something to say about the state of our coats! We walked to the side gate of the palace, with Papa limping, whilst declaring that he was fine, absolutely fine.

"Don't worry about me, children. Look after your mother. All this is hard on her. She is far from her family and she did not expect to lead such a life here."

"She has us," I said. "And Bessie."

"I know." Papa smiled and put up his hand to touch my cheek. He kissed us both and said he would see us next Sunday, if not before.

Watching him hobble towards the palace, we were filled with foreboding. How was he going to find the strength to carry on with that menial job? It was only after the door had closed behind him that I realised that I had not given him the parcel of food. I burst into tears.

Chapter 11

Gran arrived half an hour early for lunch on Sunday. She brought a bottle of wine for the adults and some chocolate for Lucy and Will.

"I know you shouldn't be eating sweets. But you've got good teeth – you get that from me. I've still got all mine. A bit of chocolate won't hurt you once in a while."

She glanced round. "Your dad not in?"

Lucy and Will looked at their mother.

"Not at the moment," she said. "Sit down, Mum. What about a wee sherry while you're waiting?"

"Wouldn't say no." Gran settled herself in an armchair. "Ranald working?"

"Not exactly."

"He can't be playing golf, surely, not in this weather?"

Their mother poured herself a sherry, took a large gulp and sat down. Lucy and Will hovered, ready to give support.

"Mum, I have something to tell you. Ranald—"

"He's not left you!"

"No, well, yes. What I mean is, he's missing."

"How can he be *missing*?"

"He is."

"So he *has* left you."

"No, not in the way you mean. He's been under a lot of stress with the business so he's gone off for a bit."

"I never did think that would work out." Gran sniffed. "What did he know about setting up a business? So it's failed, has it?"

"Seems so. Well, yes, it has."

"And he's just taken off into the wide blue yonder leaving you to clear up the mess?"

"That's not fair," Lucy burst out. "He needs time to think what to do."

"It's all right, Lucy," said her mother.

"I always thought he was far too airy-fairy about practical matters," Gran went on. She had hoped that her daughter would marry a lawyer who had been interested in her – but along had come Ranald Cunningham and swept her off her feet. That was how Gran referred to it, with a sniff, as if her daughter should have kept her balance and resisted.

"Dad's always worked hard," said Will.

"That may be so," said Gran "but to what end? I mind the time when he was selling water-purifiers. Everybody was going to want one. He would make his fortune! Buy a villa in Tuscany! Trouble was he was only paid on commission and he didn't sell many."

"The firm hadn't done its market research properly," said their mother.

"There's always some excuse. What about the service agency he set up? Talk about a hare-brained scheme! He would guarantee to find you anything you needed the minute you needed it. Someone to walk your dog. Look after your pet rabbits while you're on holiday. Water your flowers. Dig your garden. Organise your children's party. Do your weekly shopping."

"It wasn't such a bad idea," said Will. "People need these things done."

"Trouble was he didn't have anyone to do it except himself. He was running all over the town like a flea on a hot griddle."

"Have some more sherry, Mum."

Lucy and Will remembered that particular phase in their father's life. It was one they'd been involved in. They had been called on to help out at times. On one occasion Lucy was given a dog to walk. It was supposed to be a tame, quiet dog, but it had slipped its lead and run off and they'd spent half the day chasing after it until they'd had to go to the police. It was a valuable dog and was found eventually outside its own gate. There had been lots of excitement in those days.

"The very idea of him setting himself up as a business *consultant*! Helping folk to organise themselves. He couldn't organise himself out of a paper bag."

They were worried Gran might choke. Her face was growing redder by the minute, from the heat in the room and the sherry and her indignation.

"Ranald's been good to you, Mum," her daughter reminded her. "He gave you the money to go to Australia and visit Aunt Ruth."

"I know, I know. And I was grateful. I'd pay him back if I had the money. I will if I ever win the lottery. I'm just worried about the three of you."

Their father was good to everybody when he was in the money. He took his family on holiday, out to restaurants, bought them presents, lent money to friends who seldom paid it back. Where were they all now? Will wondered, then decided it wasn't fair of him to think that. His dad's friends didn't know he'd disappeared or that he was in debt. Their mum was determined to keep it quiet and had told them not to say anything about it to anyone, at least not for the meantime.

"So where has he gone?" asked Gran.

"I told you, Mum, he's missing."

"You mean you don't know? He's *really* missing?"

"I'm afraid so."

"I hope he doesn't do something stupid. I'd hate to see anything happen to him." They had known Gran would turn after she'd done her rant. Her bark was definitely worse than her bite. "I'm fond of him, Ailsa," she went on, "in spite of everything, you know that. He's a lovely man, Ranald, even if he's not much use when it comes to providing for his family."

"Let's go and eat. I'm sure you must be hungry, Mum."

When they sat down to the table Gran asked why didn't Ranald just come home? After all, it was not the first time that his business venture had failed. They weren't going to take it out on him.

"Of course not," said her daughter, carving the roast of pork. "But there is another complication."

Gran was silent once she'd heard about the debts. She shook her head and got on with her lunch. She was quiet until it came to the pudding.

"If the worst comes to the worst, Ailsa, I'll have to sell my flat," she announced.

"You can't do that!"

"What happens if he goes bankrupt? You'll be out in the street."

"We might have to sell this house. I suppose it could come to that."

That was what Lucy and Will feared.

"You can't do that – it's an heirloom," said Gran, as she poured cream over her apple crumble. "Better if I sold mine. It's nothing out of the ordinary, whereas this is."

"But you like your flat. And where would you live?"

"I'd have to come and live with you, wouldn't I?"

"Mum," said her daughter firmly, "Ranald would never allow you to sell your flat."

The doorbell rang, closing off the conversation. Will went to the door.

"I hope it's not that Smith man again," said Lucy.

They listened. It sounded as if Will was talking to a woman but they couldn't make out anything that was being said. He came back looking pale.

"Mum, it's the policewoman we saw at the station."

Their mother leapt up, as did Lucy. Gran stayed where she was.

The constable put her head round the door. "May I come in?" She had a male colleague with her.

"Of course," said their mother, flustered. "Is there any news?"

"Well, we're not sure, Mrs Cunningham, I must stress that." She looked at Will and Lucy.

"It's all right. You can say anything you have to say in front of them. And this is my mother."

"Well, as I said, we're not sure, so this could well be

a false alarm." With another glance at Will and Lucy, she said, "A body of a man, no identification papers of any kind on him, but roughly corresponding with your husband's statistics, six feet, dark hair, has been found."

"Where?" cried Lucy.

"At the foot of Salisbury Crags, in Holyrood Park."

"Holyrood Park," echoed Lucy.

Gran got up and put an arm round each of her grandchildren. Lucy had started to cry.

"There, there, love, it may not be him."

"Your grandmother's right – it may not be him."

"But it could be," said Will in a dull voice. Lucy was crying but he couldn't seem to feel anything at all. Except numbness.

The policewoman turned back to their mother. "I'll have to ask you to accompany us, Mrs Cunningham."

"Of course. I'll get my coat."

"We'll come with you," said Will.

"No, you stay with Gran. I'll get Jane to come with me."

After their mother had left with the two constables it was very quiet in the room. They all knew that she had gone to identify the body.

"Let's have a game of cards," said Gran. "We can't just sit here."

"I don't want to," said Lucy. "I don't want to do anything."

Gran ignored that and cleared the dirty dishes into the kitchen, then she fetched two packs of cards from the bureau drawer. "I'm going to teach you to play bridge. So sit yourselves down."

They sat down. She dealt the cards. They played. They were still playing when their mother returned. They ran to meet her.

"It's not Dad," she said, adding, "but it might have been. That's what's so awful." Then she burst into tears.

A little later, after they had all calmed down and his mother and grandmother had consumed a pot of tea, Will went to his room. He opened the drawer of his desk and took out the piece of paper his dad had doodled on. He stared at it, convinced, even more, that those symbols were meant to be daggers. They must be a clue as to what his father had been thinking about before he left. And the only place that could possibly throw any light on that was William and Louisa's journal.

Chapter 12

William

We decided that we would have to try to do something to help our father. If he were to continue to work as a skivvy and sleep on the floor he would end by being ill, for he has a weak chest at the best of times.

Our only contact within the palace was Tam.

"Let's ask him," said Louisa. "He might be able to help."

He had told us he'd been employed in the palace since he was a boy and knew all the Scottish noblemen who lodged there.

We went down to the Abbey Strand yesterday and hovered until he appeared. He listened sympathetically and said he would see what he could do, though he could promise nothing.

121

"Don't tell our father that we asked you," urged Louisa. "He's very proud, you see."

"I won't. I promise."

Encouraged, we went for a walk in the park. The snow had melted and the grass was green again. We turned our steps automatically in the direction of St Margaret's Loch and the chapel that sat high above it. We thought that if Papa did get a break in his duties he might well go there.

We began to scramble up the embankment and as we neared the ruin, we heard voices.

"It might be Papa." Louisa was about to surge forward but I held her back.

"I don't think it's his voice." I cocked my head. "They're talking French." Our father could speak French, but not fluently. To me, those voices – two, I thought – sounded as if they belonged to native French speakers. Our mother talked to us regularly in her own tongue so we were used to the rhythms and the way they flowed along.

We moved up a little further and crouched down, close to the ground. I was certain now that neither voice belonged to our father.

Listening carefully, we were able to follow snatches of conversation.

You must go carefully.... You will find him in the last tavern in Leith at the bottom of the Walk... He will have a paper lying on the table beside him bearing the sign of the black dagger...

We looked at each other, our eyes widening in astonishment at what we had heard. *La signe du poignard noir!*

We continued to listen.

Tell him that our plans are well advanced...

Their voices dropped after that and we could make out no more. We crept back down the bank and went to stand by the loch where we could pretend to be interested in the ducks. Pieces of jagged ice still floated in the dark water even though the weather had turned a little milder. I felt sorry for the birds on wintry days and wished we had some bread to give them. They came swimming towards us but we had to show them that our hands were empty.

In between watching the ducks we glanced up at the chapel ruin and after a few minutes saw a movement. A man emerged from behind the wall. We could not recall having seen him before. He looked as if he might be a valet. During our hours of loitering at the palace gates we had become accustomed to seeing all types of men coming and going and could generally guess what roles they had. Also, we had Peg to supply us with information.

The man came at a half-run down the bank, his knees splaying out sideways as he tried to keep his balance. From time to time he skidded a little on the slippery grass, and at one point he almost lost his foothold. He had to put a hand down to save himself from falling. Once he reached the path he walked swiftly off towards the palace.

Then the other man showed himself – and we had certainly seen him before!

Monsieur Goriot stood for a moment brushing down his coat before he, too, set off down the hill. We put our backs to him and when we risked taking a look round we saw that he was making for Croft-an-Righ where Madame de Polastron lives. We watched as he went along the lane and into her house.

"Interesting," commented Louisa. "It is a pity we can't go down to Leith and see the man in the tavern."

We were becoming as nosy as Peg herself! We were intrigued, though, to know what the two men could be plotting. *Their plans were well advanced...*

We found Peg on the Abbey Strand and Louisa gave her a poke of boiled sweets we'd brought for her. She said we were kind children and put one of the boilings into her mouth. She has only half a dozen teeth and they all look rotten.

While we were standing there we saw Madame de Polastron's son, Louis, coming down the Abbey Hill, accompanied by his valet. The boy's clothes were made of velvet and the buckles on his shoes shone in a blink of sunlight. The valet held a hand under his elbow to guide him through the patches of muck lying on the road and support him should he slip.

"He's a braw lad," said Peg. "He'll mebbe be goin' tae his dancin' class at Signor Rossignoli's."

We already knew about that, from Louisa's friend Charlotte. Charlotte attends Signor Rossignoli's dancing school in Gray's Close, as Louisa herself did before our lives changed a couple of weeks ago. Amongst the bills that we'd found was one from the dancing teacher for a year's tuition saying that if it was not paid within the next month he would have to ask Louisa to withdraw. Louisa blushed scarlet when she saw it. Whenever we pass Gray's Close now I notice that she quickens her step and looks straight ahead.

As the boy passed us he gave Louisa a smile which brought a faint glow to her cheek. According to Charlotte, he is in love with all the girls in the dancing school. Each day, when the class finishes, he waits at the bottom of the stair in order to catch them, one by one, and give them a kiss. And if they try to go past, his valet catches them and holds them for him. Louisa says that if she were there she would make sure that he did not catch her!

Our mother had been amused when we told her. "It is very French of him. And, after all, he is the son of the *comte*, so people say."

"But not his legal son," I had pointed out. "Doesn't the *comte* have two sons by his marriage?" One of them, the Duc d'Angoulême, had recently arrived at Holyrood.

"Still, he has royal blood, young Louis de Polastron."

"Well, I don't care what kind of blood he has!" Louisa had retorted. "That would not give him the right to kiss me."

Our mother thinks Louisa is sometimes too headstrong and outspoken and that neither is a desirable trait in a girl. Our father laughs and says he likes her to be spirited.

Louis de Polastron went on his way up the Canongate, attended by his valet. Louisa and I stayed on with Peg, hoping that Tam might appear again. We were not to be in luck. Once the afternoon had begun to fade we decided it was time to make for home and the heat of the fire. We felt sorry for Peg who had no fire to go to except the one in the tavern, but it was out of the question for us to take her home with us.

As we reached Gray's Close the dancing class was coming out. The girls spilled into the street, full of giggles. The boys were somewhat quieter. Charlotte left the throng and came to join us.

"He is such a lad, the French boy!" she said, her dimples deepening. I do like her very much and sometimes Louisa teases me about her.

"William," she said, "Don't you think Charlotte looks very pretty now that Louis has kissed her?"

That set them both off giggling. Girls can be very irritating. At times I want to punch Louisa and on occasions have been known to do so, a reasonably gentle one, out of the sight of our parents, of course. She can deliver a good punch back, though it happens but seldom and we make up quickly.

I looked away from the two girls to see Monsieur

Goriot standing a few yards away, at the side of the street. He must have come up the hill behind us though we had not noticed him. He appeared to be waiting for somebody.

It proved to be Louis de Polastron. Monsieur Goriot came forward when the boy emerged and greeted him.

"May I escort you home, Louis?" He spoke to him in French, of course.

I thought it odd he should come to escort Madame de Polastron's son when he already had the valet. Perhaps he was trying to curry favour. He was wearing a simpering air now, different from how we had seen him before.

He jutted out his elbow for Louis to take.

The boy accepted. "*Merci*, Monsieur Goriot."

"Don't you think he is handsome?" asked Charlotte, gazing after them.

"Who? Monsieur Goriot?" said I, pretending to misunderstand.

"Louis, idiot!"

I shrugged and Louisa smiled one of her little smiles that make me want to give her a shove. I possibly would have done had Charlotte not been with us. We walked with her to her house further up the street, in the Lawnmarket, and then went home ourselves.

Our mother was in a fuss for she had found that we were short of candles. She was telling Bessie that she must go in the morning to buy some. "They're cheaper

127

to run than the oil lamps and I am doing my very best to economise."

Bessie was trying to tell her that the candlemaker was refusing to serve her. "Nae unless he can see the colour of the money in ma haun." She rubbed her thumb and forefinger together.

"Nonsense! We have bought our candles from Mr Charles since the day I came to live in Edinburgh."

"It's true, Maman," I put in. "We were in his shop last week and he gave me this bill." I produced it from my pocket. I had neglected to give it to her or, perhaps, I had forgotten about it because I knew she would not be able to pay.

"Have him add them to the bill, Bessie," said our mother.

"We can't ask him to do that," objected Louisa.

"Besides," I said, "he *won't* do it. He asked for an early settlement. I expect he needs the money." I did not add that he has children to feed too, for that would have sounded as if I were lecturing my mother.

"You will just have to go to a different place then, Bessie. There are many other candlemakers in the town. We cannot be expected to live in the dark as well as starve."

We were not quite starving for, somehow or other, Bessie managed to produce some food for the table. Our father had left a little money which we were trying

128

to use sparingly but it must run out sooner rather than later. What would we do after that? Beg, like Peg did? No, before that, we would have to start selling some of our things. Louisa, unknown to our mother, had already returned her muff to the shop; not that that had raised any money, but at least it had cancelled out one of our smaller debts.

This morning, without saying anything, we each took some toys and half a dozen books that we'd had when we were younger. Even though we had grown past these things in age we were reluctant to part with them but knew that we must. We took the toys to the toy shop at the head of our own close. They had been bought from Mr Gray originally. Naturally he gave us less than our father would have paid, with them being second-hand. We then proceeded to Bell and Broadfoot the bookseller's in Parliament Close. We found it difficult to haggle over prices as our father might have done but in the end we had enough money to buy a box of candles.

Our mother was delighted. She did not ask how we had come by them, seeming to think that we had done what she had suggested.

"She's niver had tae manage the money hersel', that's the problem," said Bessie, when we took the candles to her in the kitchen. "Yer faither's aye protected her." Bessie did ask about the candles and when we told her she said,

"Yer mither could sell some things hersel'. They'd fetch mair money."

"That's for her to decide," I said.

We went out again after lunch and the first person we encountered was Monsieur Goriot. He was out and about in the town a great deal more than any of the other French courtiers, or so it seemed to us, who are abroad much ourselves. We did not exactly encounter him; we merely passed in the street and as we did he gave us a long stare. He could not have known, though, I reasoned, that we had been spying on him. When I glanced round I saw that he was looking back too. He did not turn until I did. And when I risked a second glance he had disappeared. He must have gone into a nearby close.

We had not long arrived at the Abbey Strand when Tam appeared. He greeted us with his usual cheery smile.

"I was hopin' I might see ye. I got yer faither a new job. He's tae wait at table."

"Oh, Tam!" Louisa hugged him and he laughed and his face reddened.

We were as pleased as if our father had been given high office in the realm.

Chapter 13

Lucy and Will had just finished reading the chapter of William and Louisa's journal when the doorbell rang. Lucy slid the book into a carrier bag lying at her feet and pushed it behind a chair while Will sprang up to go and answer the door.

"The stone, Will!" cried Lucy.

He turned back and together they lifted it up. It took a minute or two to fix it firmly into the wall. The bell rang again.

"I'm coming," shouted Will, though there was no chance anyone would be able to hear him through the thickness of these walls.

He opened the door to find one of their dad's oldest friends standing outside.

"Dan!"

"Hi, Will, how're you doing, man?"

"OK."

"Dad in?"

"No, but come on in."

Dan came in and said "Hi" to Lucy too, and then made for the radiator under the window, where he stood, warming his hands on it. "Cold out there."

"Want a cup of hot chocolate?" asked Lucy. "We were just going to have one."

"Love one. So your dad's not in? I've just been round to his office but it was all locked up. What's he playing at these days? Haven't seen him for a couple of weeks and he hasn't been answering the phone."

Lucy and Will looked at each other and nodded. They would have to let Dan know what was going on, whether their mother approved or not. She was very proud and wanted to go on pretending to the outside world that everything was normal. But it was not. Jane knew, and now Gran did. The latter was on the phone every two or three hours asking if there was any news and repeating her offer to sell her flat to pay off their debts.

"Dad's kind of disappeared," said Will.

"How do you mean *disappeared*?"

Will explained.

Dan sat down in the nearest chair. "I thought he was having problems recently, but when I asked him if there was anything bothering him – well, you know what he's like."

Will and Lucy nodded. They did. Their dad would prefer to make a joke rather than admit he had a problem.

Dan sat up straight suddenly. "Do you know, a funny thing happened to me last night. It's partly why I'm here. I was coming up the Canongate, late-ish, gone ten, and I was pretty sure I saw your dad."

"You did?" cried Louisa.

"It was dark and a bit foggy so I could easily have made a mistake. I called his name but when he didn't stop I shouted, 'Hey, pal, it's me, Dan.'"

"What did he do then?" asked Will.

"He ran off. Down a close or whatever. As I said, it was dark and murky."

"You don't know which close?"

Dan shook his head. "I thought then I must have made a mistake. But now . . ."

"But to begin with, you really did think it was him?" pressed Lucy.

"I did. I really did."

"What was he wearing?" asked Will. "Could you tell?"

Dan frowned. "Not exactly. Darkish clothing. But he was definitely wearing trainers, that I did see."

So it was certainly not the ghost of Ranald

Cunningham, born in the eighteenth century! Trainers had not been invented then. They remembered that their father had come back for his trainers, amongst other things.

"Half the men in town wear trainers," said Dan. "Though after what you've told me, I feel convinced that it was him."

"He's hiding from us," declared Will.

"Why should he want to do that?" cried Lucy.

"Maybe because he feels ashamed." Dan shrugged. "Feels he's let you down."

"We don't think that," said Lucy.

"No, but he might. I think he will."

"If only we could find him! We could tell him we don't mind."

"He must be staying somewhere nearby," said Will slowly.

But where?

They were pondering the question when their mother came home. She was as pleased to see Dan as they had been and accepted amicably the fact that they had told him about their dad. She seemed to have become resigned to the idea that the news would gradually spread. She asked Dan to stay to supper and he told her how he thought he'd seen Ranald the night before. She shook her head and said she didn't know what to think. Her head ached from thinking.

"Why don't we go out and see if there's any sign of him now?" suggested Lucy.

"You can't hang around in this weather," objected her mother. "Besides, I don't like you down there after dark."

Dan said he'd be willing to go with them. They could sit in his car and keep watch for a while. "You never know, Ranald might come out..."

Their mother was dubious. "But where on earth can he be staying?"

"What about a B&B?" suggested Lucy.

"I don't think there are any at the foot of the High Street or the Canongate, though I suppose there could be."

"A hotel?" said Dan, then he shook his head. "No, I can't imagine it."

"He wouldn't be able to afford it. I suppose he wouldn't be—"

Dan finished the sentence. "Sleeping rough? Hardly think so, Ailsa. Temperatures are dropping to below zero at night."

"Mum, let's give it a go, please," pleaded Lucy. "We don't know what else to do, do we?"

Their mother finally gave in. The inaction was getting to her as much as to them. She told them to make sure they had their mobiles with them, which meant she would phone if they were away too long. As they went out she reminded them that they had their homework to finish. What does homework matter, thought Lucy, when your dad's missing? She couldn't get a picture of him curled up in a doorway out of her head.

They chose a spot halfway down the Canongate, near where Dan had thought he'd seen their dad. Being evening, they could park on the yellow line. They settled down to wait, with Will in the front passenger seat beside Dan, and Lucy in the back, glued to the window.

"I suppose you could call this a kind of stakeout," said Will. "Like you see on the telly."

"Except that on the telly they're usually watching a specific building," said Dan.

That was the trouble: they had nothing to focus on. Every time they saw a lone man on foot approaching they sat up straight, their senses alert. But all the men went by. Only one vaguely resembled their father in height and build but by the time Will was out the door and halfway across the pavement he realised the man was a stranger. He looked back at Will, pulled up his collar and broke into a jog-trot.

It began to sleet. Dan started the engine and put on the windscreen wipers both back and front. Sleet slid down the windows, blurring the glass, leaving clear patches only where the wipers were labouring.

Lucy's mobile rang. She fished it out of her pocket but saw that the number coming up was Julie's. "I can't talk to you right now, Julie."

"Where are you?"

"I can't say."

"Why not? What's wrong with you? What are you up to these days? You're acting awful funny."

"I'll see you tomorrow."

Will's mobile then rang and their mother said, "I presume you haven't seen him? I think you should come home. Not even a dog would want to be out in this weather."

Dan conceded that she was right. "We won't find him in this."

"What if he is sleeping out?" said Lucy. "He'll freeze to death."

"I'll take a walk down later on and look into the closes," Dan promised. "I'll also go down to the Grassmarket Mission in Candlemaker Row."

The mission helped the homeless. They supposed that was what their father must be considered now.

When they got home Lucy retrieved the carrier bag that she'd put behind the chair, relieved that her mother hadn't noticed it. She went up to her room and took out the journal and called to Will to come through. She was dying to find out what happened next to William and Louisa's father but if she were to read on without Will he'd be furious.

The door closed, they sat side by side on the bed and read the next part, which had been written by Louisa.

Chapter 14

Louisa

When Papa came home last Sunday he seemed better in himself. Both William and I thought so. We presumed that waiting at table would be less exhausting than washing dishes and perhaps, too, he had found somewhere more comfortable to sleep than the scullery floor. We could not ask him.

"How long is it all to go on, Ranald?" asked our mother. "We cannot live in this way for ever more."

We had been thinking that ourselves.

"I have one or two ideas," he said vaguely.

We heard about one of them when we went down to Princes Street for a stroll in the afternoon. Our mother was not with us for she had a headache. The sun was shining and a number of people had come out to take the air. It is a fine street to walk along, being so broad and open, with a garden on one side where the Nor Loch used to be before it was drained. I looked up at the castle sitting on its rock and the tall backlands where we live spilling down the hill.

"Children," said our father, drawing us in closer to him and taking us by the arm. "I have a number of things I would like you to sell for me." He went on to give us a list: his fob watch, which had been his father's before him, a snuff box inlaid with ivory, and cufflinks with ruby studs, a present from his mother when he came of age.

"But, Papa, you can't!" I interrupted. "Not your watch! Not your cufflinks!"

"I have to," he said quietly. They won't pay off all my debts but it will be a start. And it will ease my conscience to know that some of the poor tradesmen will have their money." He added a few more items to the list. "And you must promise not to tell your mother."

"But—" I began again and, once more, he silenced me.

"She is *not* to know."

We had to promise.

He recommended us to go to a shop in the Grassmarket where he thought we would get a fair deal. "He is an honest man, Mr Beattie, but you must press him for the best price." We reminded Papa that we had once been to the shop with him. "Ah, so you have!" He then told us which of the outstanding bills he thought the money would pay. Unfortunately, there would not be enough to meet his biggest debt, the one that he was being pursued for by the messenger-at-arms with the Wand of Peace.

He sighed. "I have been very imprudent, children. You must learn a lesson from my foolish ways and not follow in my footsteps."

We pressed his hand to let him know that we loved him in spite of everything.

That evening, we made sure he left the house in plenty of time to make it comfortably back into Sanctuary before midnight. We insisted on walking with him. The messenger-at-arms and his ally were after him again. They appeared to be pursuing another man also. I tossed my head at the men as we passed them by.

We reached the sanctuary boundary well before midnight and Papa joked, saying he could have had a few more minutes at home with Maman. If we had not urged him on he would have done so. We were standing chatting when we heard shouting erupt behind us. Commotions were normal as midnight approached. The vultures gathered close to the boundary, poised to strike before the first stroke of twelve rang out. Turning, we saw a man in a brown coat go sprawling down in the roadway on the other side of the sanctuary line. At once his pursuers were on top of him. The Wand of Peace came down.

"Got you!" the men cried, their hands around his neck, half strangling him. "Got you!"

Their victorious cries made me shiver. I was thankful that we had managed to escort Papa over the line in time.

The next day, when our mother's back was turned, William and I hastily gathered up the items Papa had specified to be sold and left the house saying we were going for a walk.

"Make sure you put your hood up, Louisa," our mother called after us. "And you, William, your hat! You will get your death!"

"Yes, Maman."

We passed Bessie, who was on her way to Fishmarket Close to see if there was anything cheap going.

"And whit are the twa of ye up tae the morn?" Bessie has a suspicious mind where we are concerned.

"Nothing, Bessie," we reassured her and hurried on before she would press us further.

We went down to the Grassmarket where Mr Beattie's shop was located, feeling pleased to have got this far without arousing suspicion.

Mr Beattie's is a small, dark basement shop. Standing at the counter, half hunched over it as if to conceal what he was doing, was Monsieur Goriot!

Hearing the door open behind him, he turned sharply and when he saw us he straightened up.

"I can undertake the commission for you at the price forementioned, Monsieur Goriot," said Mr Beattie. "I know the very man who could do it for me. He is an excellent jeweller. Do you understand the terms?"

Monsieur Goriot seemed to be considering.

Mr Beattie looked round the Frenchman at us. "You are Ranald Cunningham's bairns, are you no? I thought so! And your mother, lovely lady, is French? You must be able to speak the language yersel's in that case. Perhaps you could help translate for this gentleman. I fear he doesne follow every word I have said to him."

We doubted that Monsieur Goriot would want our help and we were right. As soon as he realised what was being proposed he scooped up whatever was lying on the counter and dropped it into a bag.

"I let you know," he said in broken English and, with that, he left the shop abruptly, brushing past us without a glance.

"Strange gentleman, that," observed Mr Beattie. "He's been in before. Sometimes he's got stuff to sell. Precious stuff."

"But today he was not selling?" prompted William.

"He was wanting cufflinks made to order, with a special motif."

"What kind of motif?" I put in quickly.

"A black dagger."

William and I looked at each other and I only just restrained myself from crying out.

"Now what can I do for you?" asked Mr Beattie.

As we laid our father's treasures out on the counter top I felt my fingers shaking. I hated the thought of Papa having to part with some of the things he valued so greatly.

Mr Beattie examined each piece through his eyeglass. "Good quality," he commented, which reassured us. At least he was not going to try to pretend that what we were offering was low grade.

He made an offer and William haggled a little with him and then we settled on a price.

"You're good, lad." Mr Beattie nodded. "You won't let anyone get the better of you, I can see that."

William's face reddened but I could tell he was pleased. He can be very firm whereas I know I am inclined to waver at times.

From Mr Beattie's we went to the various shops where our father owed money and it did give us pleasure to be able to pay off each debt. It pleased the shopkeepers too!

"He's a gent, your father," said Mr Anderson the tailor at the head of the Canongate. "No ill feeling. I ken fine that he's just fallen on hard times. It kin happen to a' of us."

We saw Monsieur Goriot again, coming out of another shop. He seemed preoccupied and did not notice us. On impulse, and having completed our tasks, we decided to follow him. We had become quite intrigued by his doings. He led us along the Grassmarket towards the Cowgate until he came to a halt underneath an arch. It is a dark spot, especially when the weather is dull, which is how it was today. We pulled up short and moved back into the shadow of a doorway.

Monsieur Goriot was doing something under the arch but from our viewpoint we could not make out what it could be. After no more than two or three minutes he moved on. We waited and then when we judged the coast to be clear we left our shelter and went to investigate.

"Look!" cried William, pointing to a place high up on the wall where some kind of sign had been scrawled. "It's a dagger!"

"Monsieur Goriot must have put it there. But why?"

William was standing on tiptoe scanning the stone. "Keep watch!" he urged.

I stood where I could look in both directions. The street was quiet.

"There's something here; could be a small package," said William.

"Somebody coming!" I cried. I had just seen a man and he was coming in our direction.

William pushed the package back into the slot. We swiftly vacated the place and crossed the road.

The man stopped under the archway.

"Don't let him see that we're watching him," warned William.

I bent down and fiddled with my bootlaces and William pretended to be interested while keeping an eye on what was going on over the other side of the road.

"He's removing the package," whispered William.

When I glanced up I saw that the man had left the archway – and was coming across the road towards us!

Now that he had emerged into the light we had a clear view of him. He had a horrid red face and a bulbous nose, the kind that you see on some drunken men.

He stopped in front of us. "What're the two of ye doin' hangin' aboot here?" He was obviously not French. He was standing so close that one could see the dirt standing out in the pores of his large nose and smell the heavy ale on his breath. I wondered why Monsieur Goriot, who was a bit of a dandy, would have dealings with a man like this. I took a step back from him and hit my shoulder against the wall. "Ye're mindin' yer own business, I hope, Missie?" he went on, staring directly into my face.

"Come along, Louisa," said William, taking my hand and pulling me past.

Once we'd left the man well behind I asked William why he thought Monsieur Goriot would associate with such a person.

"Perhaps he does some dirty work for him. Perhaps the package contained money. Payment for his services."

145

I nodded. That idea seemed plausible.

There was no lack of other shady characters hanging about in the Cowgate. One or two approached us but William waved them away. One old woman, when we did not reward her with anything, cursed and spat a large gobbet of greenish phlegm right in front of us, hitting the toe of my shoe. The sight of it made me feel sick and want to cry. I know it was silly of me. Perhaps it was just that everything in our life seemed upside down, with Papa more or less imprisoned in the palace and having to sell his most precious belongings, with no way out of it all that we could see. Added to that was the feeling of menace around us. It was not surprising that we were forbidden to come into some parts of the town. Papa would not have been pleased had he been able to see us talking to a man like the one we had just met. As for Maman! We'd have had to fetch her smelling salts.

We were nearing the end of the street when we saw a woman wrapped in a dark green cloak coming out of a shop with three golden balls hanging over the doorway. The cloak looked familiar.

"Wait!" William pulled me back.

The woman crossed the road and turned up St Mary's Street.

"I'm pretty sure that was Maman," said William.

I was too.

She was not at home when we arrived there. I went

immediately to clean my boot. I wished I could throw it away but that was out of the question. I knew, though, that I would never like those boots again.

We ate unusually well this evening. We had a mutton stew with fresh baked bread and a sweet cake to follow. Only that morning, Bessie had been lamenting the fact that she had scarcely a farthing left in the housekeeping.

"Ye'll be lucky if ye eat the night," She'd told us.

I noticed that our mother was not wearing the emerald brooch of which she is so fond. She kept putting her hand up to her throat as if she expected to find it there and I remembered how we'd seen her coming out of the pawnbroker's. We had decided not to mention it unless she herself did. And she did not. Our world seems recently to have become infested with secrets.

Chapter 15

Will was still awake when the phone rang. He jumped up and ran downstairs.

"It's Dan," said his mother, covering the mouth of the telephone receiver with her hand. She was listening intently.

"Well, thanks for trying, anyway, Dan," she said after a few minutes. Her voice was flat. "Come in tomorrow if you're passing."

"No luck?" said Will.

She shook her head. "He went on foot right down the length of the Canongate, shining his torch into every close and alleyway. Disturbed one or two men wrapped in blankets and cardboard boxes. He had never seen any of them before. Then he went to the Grassmarket Mission and showed them a photograph of Dad."

"He could be sleeping in a doorway in Princes Street."

"We couldn't expect Dan to trail round the whole of Edinburgh looking in doorways."

"No, of course not."

Will went back to bed but found it difficult to sleep. He thought of his father sleeping in a doorway but somehow or other the picture didn't gel for him. Lucy had convinced herself that that must be what he was doing but Will had a feeling that his father was holed up inside somewhere. But it *was* only a feeling.

He woke up the next morning with a streaming cold, which his mother put down to hanging around in the street the night before. She said he had better stay at home. Lucy went off grumbling that she didn't feel too well either but her mother wouldn't listen.

When they had both left, Will wrapped up warmly and went out himself. He wandered down the High Street. He knew every part of it now in a way that he had never done before. Before he had often passed the mouths of the closes without even glancing in: Old Fishmarket, Fleshmarket, World's End, Mary King's, Trunk's, Anchor, and all the others.

He stopped dead – for, ahead, he saw his father. He could hardly believe it. He blinked and looked again but there was no doubt about it. It *was* his father. He was about to cross the road at the junction of the High

Street with the Bridges. For a moment Will did not move. He stood rooted to the ground, feeling as if he'd received an electric shock. Then he came alive and, shooting forward, raced down the hill. He had almost reached the junction when the lights changed and the 'red man' came on. He was going to cross, regardless of that, but a double-decker bus lumbered in front of him, forcing him back. It was a busy junction and traffic moved non-stop: buses, vans, cars. There was no space where he could even risk a crossing. He had to wait until the lights changed again.

By that time, his father was gone.

Will continued on down the street as far as the palace, even though he knew that there would be no chance of catching up with him now. He must be living somewhere in the Canongate. Why else would he be around the area so much? If he were living elsewhere he wouldn't come near this part of town. The houses that had sat hugger-mugger round the palace in olden days were mostly gone now. Only one row remained in the Abbey Strand but people didn't live there any more.

Will went into a café to think about it. He ordered a hot chocolate and sat at the window where he could watch the comings and goings in the street.

His father seemed to come out at times of the day when he thought he wouldn't be seen by them, when they would be at school and their mother at work. Or at night, after they had gone to bed. It upset him to think that his father was so set on avoiding them. He had to keep reminding himself that his dad was unwell and not himself. As Jane kept impressing on them, he was behaving irrationally. Wherever he was or whatever he was doing, it would not solve his problems, and anyone thinking straight would know that.

Will sneezed and a woman at the next table gave him a glance that made him feel as if he had rabies or yellow fever. He did feel rather conspicuous sitting there on his own.

Just then, the door opened and two women came in. One of them was his grandmother. She saw him straight away. She stopped in the doorway.

"Will, what in the name are you doing here?" she demanded. The rest of the customers had turned to look at him and a man shouted out to shut the door, for goodness' sake, it was perishing cold with it standing open.

Gran closed the door. She came over to Will's table and still standing, asked, "Why are you not at school?"

"I've got a cold."

"Shouldn't you be in your bed then?"

"I felt like some air."

"Air? It's like the Arctic out there. Does your mum know you're out?"

"No," he muttered.

"Thought not!"

He escaped as soon as he could. Just his luck to meet Gran! The whole thing had been a waste of time anyway. He walked slowly back up the street thinking about William and Louisa and the sign of the black dagger. On impulse, he took a detour down to the Cowgate. He thought he knew which archway Louisa had meant.

He stood under the arch looking around him. It was cold and dank down here. No place to be when you had a cold – that's what his gran would say. Water was dripping from overhead. He raised himself up on tiptoe. He thought he'd seen something. Putting up his hand he touched the etching of the black dagger. He smiled. It might not be of much help to him but it was reassuring in an odd way that he could not fathom. He went home.

He had just got in and was hanging up his wet anorak when the post came. They dreaded the arrival of the mail these days for it just seemed to bring nothing but letters marked REMINDER in red. This time, the postman rang the bell.

"Your mother or father in?" he asked.

Will shook his head.

"I need someone to sign."

"I could do it."

"Don't think that's on, son. You're under age. And this is an official letter."

Will felt his heart plummet.

"When will there be somebody in?"

"I think my mother should be home at lunchtime." She often came in, for a quick bite, rather than go to a café or carry sandwiches with her. "Just after one."

"I'll come back."

Will could not settle to anything after that.

His mother came bustling in a few minutes after one o'clock.

"The postie brought a letter that needed signing for," Will told her straight away. "He's coming back."

No sooner had he spoken when the postman was at the door again.

"Sign here please, Mrs Cunningham. And print your name below."

She signed and the postman left. She carried the envelope into the living room. It was addressed to her husband but she intended to open it. Will stood beside her.

She withdrew the sheet of paper and took a deep breath before looking at it. It was a writ, served on Mr Ranald Cunningham by MacAtee, MacPherson and Trimble Financial Services, for the sum of fifty thousand pounds. He was given fourteen days to reply.

"What are we going to do?" asked Will. "He's not here to reply."

"I don't know. I'll see if Jane is free later."

After his mother had gone back to work Will looked up the Yellow Pages telephone directory. He found MacAtee, MacPherson and Trimble. They had a big ad, offering loans for any purpose up to two hundred thousand pounds. You could get the money on the same day and you didn't even have to give any proof of your income. That was how his dad had been able to do it. He'd had no income. The only condition appeared to be that you owned your own house.

"That's how they can get their money back," said Jane, when she came round that evening. "If you don't pay they'll try to force the sale of the house."

"What'll happen if dad doesn't reply?" asked Will.

"They can go for a decree for payment in the Sheriff Court in his absence."

They were staring glumly at the writ when Dan arrived. He said he wished he could be of help. He'd lend them something if he could. "But I haven't got that kind of money."

None of them did.

"You could take out a mortgage on the house, Ailsa," suggested Dan.

"We've already done that," she said. "Ranald used the money to set up the business."

"You might be able to increase it."

"Possibly." She frowned. "I don't know if I'd be able to meet the payments though. And I've no intention of getting into debt myself!"

"That's the last thing you want to do," said Jane.

Lucy's mobile rang. It was Julie. Lucy went out into the lobby to answer it.

"You couldn't come round for an hour, could you?" Julie lived ten minutes' walk away. "My mum's out and I'm in by myself." Julie and her mum lived on their own, just the two of them.

"I'm coming," said Lucy. She needed to get out of the house. All this talk of money and debts and their house being sold was doing her head in. Her mother was so distracted by it all that when Lucy said she was going out she didn't even protest, just said absentmindedly, "Don't be late."

Lucy ran before she could be called back.

Chapter 16

William

We have much to record! Events have moved fast this week, especially in the last twenty-four hours.

We are growing more and more interested in Monsieur Goriot. Our paths cross regularly since we are always out and about and so is he. Once one starts deliberately looking for a person one sees him everywhere. We see him escorting Louis de Polastron around the town, simpering in most sickening fashion while he talks to the boy. We see him, too, meeting odd characters on corners and exchanging only a few words with them, or sometimes not even that.

Peg keeps telling us that the French are about to invade Scotland and the town is full of their spies. We never know how much of Peg's stories to believe. As Louisa says, Peg likes to embroider. But it is true that people are worrying about a French invasion. Some say their ships are standing out to sea off the Scottish coast, others that their troops are advancing over the border from England. The rumours pass from mouth to mouth up the street and down the closes. A regiment called the Royal Edinburgh Volunteers has been formed to defend the city and men are being urged to enlist. They have blue uniforms with red facings and because of that are known as the 'True Blues'.

Our mother is in a flap. The very thought of the army of that fiend Napoleon Bonaparte advancing into Edinburgh!

"You do not realise what this will mean, *mes enfants*. They hate the aristocracy. They will send them to the guillotine, just as they did my poor king and queen."

"They won't touch us, Maman," Louisa told her. "We are poor."

"But I come from a good family in France."

Louisa and I do not think Napoleon and his men would know that.

"You would not want fine men like the Duke of Hamilton to be taken to the guillotine, would you?"

Of course we would not. We would not want anyone to suffer that and cannot understand the people who go to watch executions down in the Grassmarket or at the Girth

Cross. Our father thinks that those who do are the very dregs of society, feeding on the ills and grief of others.

When he came home on his last weekly visit he said he did not think the invasion was quite so imminent or certain. He was also of the opinion that if there were to be one it was unlikely that Napoleon would lead it since he was much too busy waging war in Italy. There is much talk of it in the palace amongst the French *emigrés*, however. Papa told Maman that, at least, she could relax and forget about Boney the Bogeyman!

"You are such an *optimiste*, Ranald," said our mother. "You never take things seriously enough, not until it is too late."

That is probably true. Our father is always inclined to wait and see what will happen and not worry until it does. We have begun to feel that he has settled too much into being an 'abbey laird'. He has been given employment as a valet, because, we think, he has been judged to be of good character. Also, he speaks French, which must be an advantage in the palace nowadays. He told the two of us about his new employment, sounding rather pleased with himself. We are keeping it to ourselves. Our mother still thinks he is a right-hand man of the count's and we do not see any point in telling her otherwise.

About the possibility of war, we – that is Louisa and I, and our friends – are uncertain what to think. We feel some shivers of fear at the thought of an invasion, and some, I confess, of excitement. Charlotte's father has joined the True Blues and I wish I were old enough to do so myself. Louisa says she is glad I am not. She does not like the idea of me fighting.

With all these rumours flying around, the Town Guardsmen have started to emerge at intervals from their wooden shed opposite the Old Tollbooth and parade up and down the street in their shabby red uniforms and cocked hats to show us that they are alert. They are mostly Highlanders and some of them carry a Lochaber axe instead of a musket. The townspeople lampoon them and call them the 'town rottens' or 'rats'; Bessie says we will all be dead in our beds if we have to rely on them to protect us from Boney. She is sure they wouldn't know how to fire a musket if they tried. They would probably shoot themselves in the foot. They are able to beat the drum for the ten o'clock closing of the taverns but not much more than that.

According to Peg, French spies have come in amongst the supporters of the count. We have begun to think, judging by his behaviour, that Monsieur Goriot might be one of them. But how are we to prove it? And even if we do, what could we do with the information? Nevertheless, we are keeping up our surveillance of him and we took Charlotte into our confidence so that she can be a lookout too. She has become friendly in the dancing class with Louis de Polastron, which I do not care for very much, although I realise that the connection might be useful. Louis talks to her because she understands a little French. Louisa and I have been giving her lessons.

Charlotte was able to tell us that the Comte d'Artois is a frequent visitor at Madame de Polastron's house, going there often in the evening to play cards. Also, that Monsieur Goriot is always coming around trying to get into favour with Louis' mother, who appears to be in poor health much of the time. "Louis doesn't like him," said Charlotte. "I daresay his poor mother could do without Monsieur Goriot pestering her."

"I don't see how anyone could like Monsieur Goriot," said Louisa.

"I'll see what else I can find out," Charlotte promised. "It is good fun being a spy!" Her eyes sparkled and I confess that I did think she looked uncommonly pretty.

We are also finding it fun. It gives a little edge of excitement to the day.

When we were tracking Monsieur Goriot down into the Grassmarket this morning, he stopped suddenly and waited until the three of us caught up with him.

"Are you following me?" he asked, taking a step closer to us. "You are, aren't you? I do think you are. And you speak French, so don't pretend that you don't understand me! What are you about?"

"We are doing an errand for our friend's mother," said

Louisa, ignoring his questions. And, indeed, it was true for we were to go to Mr Cowan the candlemaker's to buy candles for Charlotte's mother. We were glad it was not Mr Charles for we would not have liked to show our faces there. We have still not paid his bill.

"I see you around all the time," said Monsieur Goriot. "What is it you want with me?"

"Nothing," I returned. "We like to walk about the town."

He thought for a moment, whilst wrinkling his nose and pursing his lips, before saying, "I don't like being followed by nosy children. Remember that, won't you? I have friends who don't like them, either. You understand me, don't you?"

We did, very well. He was threatening us. I thought of the man with the bulbous nose whom he'd met down in the Cowgate. I was sure he could be vicious if called upon.

"I would be very sorry if you children were to come to any harm," said Monsieur Goriot in a soft, mocking voice, and then he left us.

"What did he say?" asked Charlotte, after he had gone, for she had not understood everything he'd said.

"He doesn't like us following him," I said, not wishing to worry her. "Shall we go and buy your Mama's candles?"

Mr Cowan served Charlotte willingly for her father, apart from being a member of the True Blues, is a solicitor-at-law and pays his bills on demand. I carried the candles for her. It seemed only right since I am stronger.

Papa always insists that I behave like a gentleman, especially to ladies. Sometimes I fear I do not where Louisa is concerned. But then she is my sister; my twin! She smirked when I took the box from Charlotte's hands and I felt like giving her a kick on the shin.

After we had walked Charlotte home and delivered the candles, Louisa and I continued on down the hill to Holyrood, hoping to see our father. Sometimes, now that he is a valet, he is able to come out around midday after he has completed his morning duties. We had been waiting only a few minutes when he appeared.

"Shall we walk in the park?" he suggested.

We love these times with him. It is as if they are stolen hours.

We entered by Croft-an-Righ and, passing the house of the Polastrons, whom should we see going in but Monsieur Goriot! For once he did not see us. We told Papa we didn't like the man and that we had seen him meeting suspicious-looking characters in shady places.

"Strange you should say that, but I get the same feeling about him. He always seems to be creeping about the palace eavesdropping."

I resolved then and there that we ought to do something more positive about finding evidence against Monsieur Goriot. I said nothing, though, to Papa.

"I think you should stay away from him, children," he said, as if reading my mind. "If he is involved in something dubious he will stop at nothing. Men like him have no scruples."

The opportunity to act came more quickly than I had thought. Later in the afternoon, we went out for another walk, hoping we might see our father again, but we did not. We saw, instead, our quarry, in the Abbey Strand. He had just come out of a tavern. We held back in a doorway and watched.

Monsieur Goriot hovered around for a few minutes. He seemed to be looking for someone. Sighting a caddie, he signalled to him. We know the caddie. His name is Lecky and he has often taken messages for our father. Monsieur Goriot put an envelope and some money into Lecky's hand and spoke to him. Lecky nodded and Monsieur Goriot turned and walked at a rapid pace towards the palace.

We emerged from the shadows and I hailed Lecky.

"Ah, Master William," he said, "and young Miss Louisa! I'm right sorry aboot yer faither's troubles. He'll be a sair miss tae ye."

We agreed wholeheartedly. We chatted to Lecky for a few minutes and Louisa asked after his children. He has several and they live in one room in the Cowgate. Our mother gives them our cast-off clothes.

"I'm goin' yer way," he said. "I'll walk wi' ye. I have tae deliver this tae an address up by the castle." He waved the envelope. "I was just on my way home but I couldne turn awa' a bawbee, could I now?" Well, a halfpenny is better than nothing.

"We could deliver it for you, Lecky," I said on impulse. "It would save you a walk."

"Well, I dinne ken," he said doubtfully, but it was starting to rain quite hard and he was wearing only a thin jacket and his shoes were cracked across the front.

"It wouldn't be any trouble," I insisted. "Truly it wouldn't."

"We'd be happy to, Lecky," added Louisa. "You'll get soaked in this rain."

Even as she spoke, it was beginning to turn to a fine sleet.

"It's fer Riddle's Court," he said.

"That's not much further on than us," I said. "Only a step or two. It would be no bother."

"Weel, if ye're sure?" He was still sounding uncertain and I was worried he might not agree.

"Of course!" I replied.

I held out my hand and he put the envelope into it.

Chapter 17

Reluctantly, Will put the journal back into the cavity in the wall and together they replaced the stone. Their mother was due in shortly. One day, perhaps when they got to the end of William and Louisa's story, they would tell her about it.

"I can't wait to find out what's in Monsieur Goriot's envelope," said Lucy. "Do you think they'll open it?"

"I would!" said Will.

For the moment, though, they were more concerned about the envelope containing the writ for their father. It had been lying on the kitchen table for six days now so they had only eight left in which to find him. Or for him to turn up. But as the days passed, that seemed less and less likely. After Will had caught sight of him down the High Street they had been half hoping that the front door might open unexpectedly and they'd hear his voice cry out, "Hi, folks! It's me, Dad! I'm home."

Their mother thought the longer he stayed away the more difficult it would be for him to come back. Dan had been doing a nightly trawl down through the Canongate and Cowgate but with no success. As he said, it was as if their dad had vanished into thin air.

Their mother came in and they ate and chatted and tried to pretend that everything was normal. Their father wasn't mentioned. Afterwards, Will and Lucy settled down to their homework.

"Would you mind if I popped out to meet Jane for half an hour?" asked their mother. "No going round to Julie's now, Lucy!" she added on the way out. The last time Lucy had gone she'd got a row for being late.

They finished their homework.

"What do you feel like doing?" asked Will. "There's nothing on the telly."

Lucy shrugged.

They were feeling empty. It was as if their life had a great big hole in the centre of it and there wasn't anything more they could do about it. They had racked their brains, searched everywhere they could think, strained their eyes scanning faces in the street and knew every close and alley backwards. After all that, they still had no lead whatsoever.

"Let's get the journal out again," said Lucy. "We might as well see how William and Louisa are getting on."

They went to fetch it.

Chapter 18

Louisa

After we left Lecky the caddie we went home. We walked behind Leerie as he made his way up the street with his long pole. The lights came on one by one ahead of us, lighting our steps. Glistening through the sleet they looked almost ghostly. William had put Monsieur Goriot's envelope into his pocket and was keeping his hand over it, as if he was afraid that it might fall out or be snatched. I had no idea whether he intended to deliver it, or not. He had his head down and was watching the road unfold beneath his feet. I sensed he was turning the problem over in his head, as I was. We did not speak.

Halfway up the hill, we were surprised to meet Charlotte.

"My mother asked me to take a potion to my aunt. She is unwell." Charlotte's hood was rimmed with drops of moisture. I was sure my hair, which was uncovered, must be soaking wet. I would get a row from Bessie when we got in.

"Any news?" asked William. "Did you see Louis today?"

Charlotte nodded and we moved into the shelter of a doorway with her.

"Did he have anything to tell you?" I asked.

"Only that the Comte d'Artois is coming to play whist with his mother this evening."

"He often does, doesn't he?" I said. It did not seem a very interesting piece of information.

"But tonight Monsieur Goriot is coming too. It seems he has managed to worm his way into Madame de Polastron's affections."

We did not think much about that just then. We talked to Charlotte for a few minutes until, finding that our feet were beginning to freeze, we parted and went our separate ways. The sleet was thickening by the time we reached our close-mouth and we could scarcely see a foot in front of us. We did not stop to discuss whether or not we should continue on up to Riddle's Court to deliver the letter. We skidded down the steps into the house where Bessie awaited us, ready to fuss. She wanted to remove our coats but William moved away and put his back to her and I saw, out of the corner of my eye, that he removed the envelope from his coat pocket and slid it inside his shirt.

Our mother came out of the living room, throwing up her hands. "*Mon dieu!* What have you been doing out there, children, *mes enfants*? You wring with water. Look, you puddle on the floor! Come into the fire!"

William, instead, dashed up the stairs muttering that he had to collect something.

"I'll be back in a minute, Maman," I said, throwing off my cloak, and then I went after him before she could stop me.

He was standing in the middle of his room with the letter in his hand. It was sealed with black wax.

"Come and see!" he said. "It has been stamped with the sign of the black dagger."

"It must be a secret society, mustn't it?" I said, feeling a thrill run up my spine and make my neck twitch. I shivered.

Once the seal was broken it would be impossible to repair it and the letter could not then be delivered. And if Monsieur Goriot were to find out that it had not been, he would be furious with Lecky, whom we would not wish to harm.

"Are we going to open it?" I asked.

"We have to! It's our chance to see what Monsieur Goriot is up to."

"If anything," I cautioned. After all, it was possible that

the Frenchman might belong to some sort of society that likes to keep itself secret but is not involved in anything criminal. We believe there are a number of drinking and gambling societies.

"I know." William nodded. "It might just be an invitation to join them for whist at Madame de Polastron's this evening."

"Who is it addressed to?"

"Monsieur Vauquer." So, another Frenchman.

Without another word, William broke the seal and I felt my heart race. He removed a slip of paper. At the top was the drawing of a black dagger.

The message was quite short, and in French, with no signature: *C'est ce soir. 10 h. Porte de derrière. Voiture attend. Et trois amis.*

"Maybe it is just an invitation to play whist." I felt let down. I had hoped for something more dramatic, more definite.

"I think it's more than that," said William slowly, frowning as he studied the piece of paper. "Why would he say *porte de derriere*? The back door?" He read the message aloud, in English. "It's this evening. Ten o'clock. Back door. Carriage awaits. And three friends." He looked up. "Where does the carriage wait? Which back door? And who are the three friends?"

"They wouldn't start to play whist as late as ten o'clock, would they?"

"They might. But I wouldn't think so."

We would not – but we did not know the ways of the aristocracy. Perhaps the count liked to play late into the night; though, according to Peg, the lights were usually out by midnight in Madame de Polastron's house.

We were mulling all this over when we heard Bessie's voice shouting to us from below. "Yer tea's poured. It's gettin' cauld."

William put the letter back into the envelope and placed it under his pillow.

We drank our tea but our minds were not on our mother's conversation. She had had a letter from a relative in France bemoaning the state of her country. "She tells me I am the lucky one not to be there. The present government is cruel. *Tout est horrible!* They want the monarchy back. They want the Comte d'Artois' brother Louis for king."

"Not everyone does, I think," said William. "Papa says the poor may well do better under a republic. It was because there was so much poverty and misery that there was a revolution. He says that's why most revolutions start."

"What does he know about it? He has never lived through one."

"He reads," I said.

"And he thinks," added William.

"It is a pity he cannot *act* at times." Our mother sighed.

"Your Papa is a dear man and so very romantic but, *mes enfants*, you must agree that he is not terribly *useful*, not for ordinary things of the day?"

Bessie put her head round the door. "I'm awa now, Mam."

"Where are you going, Bessie?" I asked.

"To see my sister. She's nae weel."

"Stay with her overnight, Bessie," said our mother. "We can manage without you till morning."

"Thank you, Mam."

Bessie departed. We were to find her absence useful.

She had left us broth for supper. There was much barley and little meat in it. After we had eaten I washed up the plates even though Maman said I could leave them for Bessie in the morning. It took only a few minutes and it would please Bessie.

"What about a game of cards?" suggested our mother.

We drew the green baize-covered card table up close to the fire and Maman dealt. It always cheers her to play cards. William and I, once again, could not keep our minds on what we were doing so that she won every game. We were glad when it was time to fold up the table. I yawned and said I was tired and might go to bed.

"It is but eight thirty," said Maman, looking at her watch. "You are early tonight." Most evenings, she has to prompt us.

It was only when she had looked at her watch that I

realised that the French ormolu clock which normally sat on the mantelpiece was missing.

She saw my eyes go to the space. "I sold it this morning," she said. "I got very good price for it."

She had been very fond of that clock. It had been given to her by her grandmother when she married our father. I wondered how many more things we were going to have to sell. I got up and went to Maman and gave her a kiss.

"I'm sure Papa will find an answer soon to our problems," I said.

She sighed and said she would not be long out of her bed tonight either.

William kissed her also and we went upstairs. I followed him into his room and he took out Monsieur Goriot's letter and we read it yet again.

"Something is obviously going to happen at ten o'clock this evening," said William. "What, we don't know, but something, whether good or bad."

From what we knew of Monsieur Goriot, we did not think it could be good.

"He is summoning his friend Monsieur Vauquer," William went on, summing up, "to come to a back door where a carriage and three friends will be waiting. It would help to know *which* back door."

"We do know that Monsieur Goriot is going to Madame de Polastron's this evening," I reminded him.

"Yes, we do." William considered. "I think we have to go

out, Louisa, once Maman has gone to bed. First, though, she must think we are asleep. Wait in your room until I come for you."

I did as he said and got into bed, fully clothed, except for my boots. A few minutes later, when Maman opened the door and put her head in to say goodnight, I murmured back in a sleepy voice. I lay still and listened while she went to William's room and then her own. After a little while the house fell silent and I risked getting up.

William opened my door and signalled to me. We crept down the stairs in our stockinged feet. I missed the ticking of the French clock. The silence in the house seemed almost deathly. At the bottom of the stairs we put on our boots. William lifted his heavy coat from the peg and I my cloak. We were ready for the night.

It was a cold one and the ground was greasy underfoot. A thin curtain of sleet was still falling but I thought that perhaps that might help to shroud us from passing eyes. Also, it was keeping people indoors. There was no sign even of the Town Guard who must be lying low in their barracks. We passed a drunkard lurching along. He did not notice us.

The Tron clock showed that it was fifteen minutes past nine o'clock. In forty-five minutes Monsieur Vauquer was expected to come to the back door of a house but of course he did not know this so he would not come. The three friends and the carriage, however, should be waiting.

When we reached the foot of the Canongate we stopped in the lee of a building and I asked William what we were going to do.

"Talk to Papa. He is good at thinking, after all." And we did not know what to think. "But, first, let us go and see if there is a carriage waiting near the Polastron house. If there is we must be careful not to let them see us or the game will be up."

The Abbey Strand was quiet, though there would still be people inside the taverns since it was not yet ten. Beyond the strand stood the dark outline of the palace, shrouded in a white mist. The sleet had thickened and was turning to snow. We rounded the corner into Abbey Hill and William put his arm through mine to help steady me. It was treacherous underfoot. My eyelashes were becoming caked with flakes, almost blinding me, so that I had to keep fluttering them. I felt as if I were walking through a thick, damp, swirling fog. It was difficult to know, too, if we were keeping firmly to the road. Once or twice we stumbled, only narrowly avoiding falling into a ditch.

When glimmers of light began to appear we decided that we must be near Croft-an-Righ. Those must be the windows of Madame de Polastron's house.

There was no sign of a carriage on the road. We halted.

"It could be the back door of any house," I said, or shouted rather, for the wind was howling. It was no night for man nor beast to be abroad, as Bessie would have said.

176

"Let's go on a bit. You never know, the carriage might be further along. It would be too obvious if it were sitting at the entrance of Croft-an-Righ."

Clinging together, we moved on again. After we had gone a few yards we gradually began to make out something large and dark in the road ahead of us. A vehicle of some kind possibly. A *carriage*? If so, there might be people in it. *Les trois amis?*

We edged forward, very slowly, and as we drew closer we were able to discern the outline of a black, closed carriage, with two black horses standing between the shafts.

"Wait there," said William. "Don't move."

Stooping low, he crept up to the back of the carriage. I wondered how long he would stay there – for it seemed ages though it was probably only seconds. I was terrified that the carriage door would swing open at any moment and a man would jump out and find him.

William came back.

"It has the sign of the black dagger on the back," he said.

Chapter 19

Their heads close together, bent over the journal, Will and Lucy finished the page and turned over, their own father and his troubles forgotten for now. They *had* to find out what was going to happen to the Comte d'Artois, as well as to the father of Louisa and William.

Chapter 20

William

One of the black horses was neighing and pawing the ground. It was obviously growing restless. The weather was severe for even a horse to stand about. We could not make out if there was anyone inside the coach. If there were, and we were to go closer to try to find out, we might invite disaster. Nothing, except the horse, seemed to be stirring. I thought of the company playing cards in Madame de Polastron's house, and how the count might be sitting there unaware that he was at risk. For I felt fairly sure that he must be.

"Come on!" I said. "There can't be much time left. We need to fetch help!"

We turned back towards the palace, going as fast

as we could on the treacherous ground. Running was impossible. At one point, Louisa almost lost her footing and I had to hold tightly on to her, and in the next moment I myself almost went headlong.

Once at the palace, we had to find a way to gain entrance. I thought our best chance would be to ask for Tam.

We went to a side door where we were stopped by a guard. When we asked to speak to Tam Brunton we were told that he had gone out. We would probably find him in the White Horse Tavern in the close of the same name near the foot of the Canongate.

We ran all the way, slipping and sliding. The inn is at the back of the close, with houses lining the two sides. I said Louisa should wait as I intended to go in alone. Taverns are no place for women or girls. Or boys possibly, either. Our mother would have had hysterics if she could have seen me. As I pushed open the door the heat and noise struck me full force in the face. I could hardly see through the fug of tobacco smoke but at least the place was warm, being packed from wall to wall with customers drinking up before the drum beats would sound. I wove my way through the drinkers, scanning faces to right and left. One or two men swore and informed me that I had no business to be here.

I was relieved when I caught sight of one familiar face. Peg was sitting in a corner with a tankard in her hand. "Whit are ye daein' here, laddie?"

She helped me to find Tam, who was in the other room. He left at once to come with me once I'd told him that we thought the Comte d'Artois might be in danger. There was no time for explanations. We joined Louisa and hurried across to the palace. The guard allowed us to pass and we went quickly along the corridor and up three flights of stairs to a small boxroom where we found our father lying on a straw pallet reading a book by the light of a candle. He leapt up, astonished to see us.

"Listen, Papa," I said and then related as briefly as I could what we had found out. "So you see, we think Monsieur Goriot is plotting something."

"From the sound of it, they might well be planning to kidnap the count!"

"That's what we're afraid of."

"Bonaparte's supporters would like rid of all the members of the French royal family. They're worried they might try to reclaim the throne. We must act at once!"

Our father took charge. It was a long time since we had seen him so purposeful. Walking briskly, he led us back along the corridor, talking as he went. "Tam, go and alert the guard. Children, you go home and stay in the house!"

There was no way whatsoever that we would do that. Both Tam and our father had ceased to notice what we were doing. They were striding ahead and had soon disappeared into the nether regions of the palace to summon help. We slipped back out into the street, stopping to ask the guard if he knew what time it was. Seven minutes before ten, he was able to tell us. *Seven minutes to!*

We half walked, half ran, half slid back up Abbey Hill. The snow had thinned and the sky must have cleared at least partially, for a three-quarter moon had come out and was lighting the ground in front of us. We came to a stop before we got as far as Croft-an-Righ, arrested by what we saw ahead of us.

Three men, dressed in black, walking stealthily and hunched over, as if they wished to conceal themselves, were turning into the lane... *Trois amis*. Three friends.

Once they'd disappeared, we moved up. But before we reached the lane we heard a shot. Somebody had fired a musket!

Shouts and cries now filled the air. We rounded the corner into Croft-an-Righ and carried on to the Polastron house. We gasped. The three men in black, along with Monsieur Goriot, with black daggers at their belts, and muskets drawn, were conducting the Comte d'Artois out of the house! We had been too late fetching help.

The count was trying to protest but the men were urging him on, brandishing their weapons. Madame de Polastron stood in the lit doorway wrapped in a shawl, waving her arms frantically and protesting, also.

Behind her, we saw the white, shadowy face of her son Louis.

On the ground, at the side of the door, lay a man sprawled face downwards, his legs and arms splayed out. He looked like a guard. He looked dead.

Turning, Monsieur Goriot spied us.

"Ah, so it's you two again," he said in his soft, slimy voice as he came towards us. He tossed his musket to one of the other men and took the dagger from his belt. "Go over there!" he barked, his voice no longer soft, and he pointed the dagger straight at my heart. I was so petrified that I felt frozen. Louisa screamed.

Then Monsieur Goriot cocked his head. He thought he could hear something. So did we.

In the next moment, a posse of palace guards was upon us.

"Get out of the way!" a voice shouted.

We ducked as a shot was fired and fled into the bushes where we huddled, clutching each other. A fierce battle ensued, at the end of which all four of the would-be kidnappers and two of the palace guards lay dead. I could feel Louisa retching and thought she might be sick. She took a couple of deep breaths and calmed herself. I did not feel so very calm myself.

"Louisa! William!" It was our father calling, his voice urgent.

We emerged from the bushes, scratched, wet and

183

trembling. We fell into Papa's arms and he held us close against him.

We were invited into the Polastron house and given hot chocolate. The count was sitting by the fire drinking a glass of brandy and recovering from his ordeal. Madame de Polastron was fussing over him, as was another lady who was present. Once Tam had explained that it had been us who had raised the alarm, the count was full of gratitude. He said that he wished that he could reward us in some way. We rather did too, for it would be helpful, but we knew he had no money.

I thought suddenly of Monsieur Vauquer, the man to whom Monsieur Goriot's letter had been addressed. He must have been in the plot too. I told the count about him and the letter which we had not delivered and he straight away instructed the captain of the guard to take some men and make haste to Riddle's Court to arrest the Frenchman.

Some of the Scottish nobles who lodged in the palace arrived, having heard of the fray, and they too thanked us. We basked in the heat of Madame de Polastron's fire and also, I have to admit, the praise of these noble men. The count said that we must come and visit him at the palace and bring our mother, whom he would very much like to meet, especially since she was a fellow countrywoman. We knew that would please her. It also reminded us that she might be awake and worrying about us. She often sleeps badly and gets up in the night.

"I will walk you up the hill," said our father. "I won't let you go alone at this hour."

"But you can't, Papa!" I said, wishing that he could come home with us now and stay there. "You might be arrested."

No doubt, with all this happening, the Town Guard would be out, and Papa was still listed as a debtor.

"I will walk them home," offered one of the Scottish nobles.

"That would be most kind," said our father.

We took our leave of the assembled company and set off for home. Our escort walked between Louisa and me, giving an arm to each of us. He told us that the count was a very special friend and said that he could not thank us enough for having saved his life. He felt sure that Monsieur Goriot and his men, once they had kidnapped him, would have killed him.

"You are both exceedingly brave."

"Not really," said Louisa. "I was terrified. I thought Monsieur Goriot was going to run William through with his dagger."

"Fortunately he did not!" We passed from the Canongate into the High Street. "You have fallen on hard times of late, I think?" our escort continued.

We agreed that that was so.

"I shall see if I can do something for your father."

"Oh, would you?" cried Louisa. "We want him to come home so very badly!"

"I will see what I can do."

The nobleman insisted on coming down the close with us to our own door. We said goodnight and thanked him; and I hoped that he would not forget his promise.

Our mother was up. She had been tearing her hair to pieces for the last hour, she informed us. She had looked into our rooms and found our beds empty.

"You are very bad children to do this. You have put me through a thousand agonies. I have been distraught and I did not even have Bessie here!"

"We were saving the life of the Comte d'Artois," said Louisa.

"You were doing *what*?"

"Sit down, Maman," I said, "and we will tell you all about it."

She almost fainted when she heard that we had been so close to danger, and Louisa had to fetch her smelling salts. But by the time we had finished our story she was saying how brave we were and how thrilled she was to know that the Comte d'Artois, brother to the heir of the French throne, had invited us to the palace.

We slept late this morning, after all the excitement of last night. Bessie was back by the time we got up and was making porridge. She had heard the news. The whole town had heard!

"What clever children I have, Bessie," said our mother, putting a hand on each of our shoulders. "Now, if only their father could come home we might be a happy family again!"

We thought there might be a chance that he soon would but we said nothing for we did not know if the nobleman would be able to pay our father's debts even if he would wish to. Some of the Scottish nobles did not seem to be much better off than the count himself.

As soon as we had eaten we were off down the hill again. Peg was outside the palace gates.

"Ye're the toast o' the toun," she told us.

The guard allowed us to enter the palace once we had explained who we were. We were being treated like royalty itself!

We found Tam first and he took us to our father, who was sitting in a room with our friend from yesterday. They both rose as we came in and the nobleman shook our hands. He told us first of all that Monsieur Vauquer had been arrested as he was attempting to flee. We were delighted with the news.

"There was a little cell of them, bent on wiping out what is left of the monarchy. They called themselves the Black Daggers. But I think you found that out for yourselves? What clever children you have, Ranald!"

That was the second time we'd been complimented so. Our father was smiling. I wondered if he would say we were not so much clever as nosy!

The nobleman went on to tell us that he was on the point of leaving for Leith where he would embark for Rotterdam. He had urgent business to attend to on the continent. He hinted that it might even have something to do with the Black Daggers. He thanked us warmly again for the part we had played in saving the count and said that he hoped our paths would cross sometime in the future. Then he left.

We felt a little flat after he had gone and I wondered if he would have had time to do anything for our father. But Papa was still smiling and I noticed that he had some papers in his hand.

"Has he given you some money?" we asked simultaneously.

Our father nodded. "I was extremely reluctant to take it—"

"Oh, Papa!" To think that he might have refused! Our father is a very proud man and we admire him for that but we think that sometimes, perhaps, one can be too proud. Sometimes one needs help. He is loath to admit that.

"I thought under the circumstances, though, that I should," he continued, "so that I can be a proper father to you again. The money I have been given will pay my debts."

I wondered why the nobleman had not paid off the debts of the Comte d'Artois but, of course, our father's were small in comparison.

"I have already sent a messenger to do so," our father continued.

We flung our arms around him.

"Not only that," he went on, "our friend has given us an apartment."

"In the palace?" asked Louisa.

"No, no, nothing so grand. It is a very small one, apparently, just a couple of rooms, quite nearby. I have the deeds here and he has sent instructions to his solicitor."

"What is our friend called?" I asked.

"Lamont. Whether it is his surname or his Christian name, I have no idea. It could be either. But that is what we are to know him by."

"What shall we do with the apartment?" asked Louisa. "We already have a house."

I thought of Peg but I was not sure that our father would agree to her living there. Nor did I think she might want to. She had told us she'd spent so much of her life outside that she felt restless when she was stuck inside four walls for long.

"It's a kind of hideaway," said our father. "Lamont called it a safe haven. He has asked that we keep it a secret within the family for he may come at times to use it himself. He has retained a key."

"He seems to be a man of mystery." I imagined him having secret assignations in Rotterdam and other places on the continent, in the way that Monsieur Goriot had, but I hoped that his would be in aid of good causes. I could only think they would be. He had seemed a man of honour.

"I asked no questions of him," said our father. "We are each entitled to keep secret what we wish in our lives. I think he is much involved with the French royal family." He held up a key. "Shall we go and look at it?"

It felt wonderful to be able to cross over the sanctuary boundary with our father and know that he was a free man and not in danger of being tapped on the shoulder with the Wand of Peace. He led us past the Girth Cross, and at the foot of the Canongate we turned into White Horse Close where we had been only the previous evening looking for Tam. Papa led us up a stair, stopped at a door, inserted the key in the lock, and we went inside.

The apartment was small but cosy and furnished with a sofa – which could be used as a bed, I saw – a table, and two upright wooden chairs. A couple of bright Oriental rugs lay on the floor. Apart from that, there was only a cupboard and a kitchen which held but a small range and some utensils.

"I like it," said Louisa.

And so did I.

"There is one condition attached," said our father. "It is to be written into the deeds that the owner will not tell his children about this place until he judges that they are of an age to be entrusted with the secret."

"We are of that age now," I said.

"You are," agreed our father. "And so the secret is now in your care. Shall we go home and see your mother?"

Chapter 21

Will and Lucy closed the book and looked at each other.

"Do you think...?" said Lucy.

"That Dad might be there?" said Will. "Let's go and find out!"

They left a note for their mother, saying merely that they had gone out, then they seized their anoraks and ran from the house. They did not stop running until they reached the lower Canongate. There they paused to catch their breath and to wonder in what state they would find their father, *if* they did find him.

"He might not want to see us," warned Will.

"He's going to have to," said Lucy fiercely.

"Let's go then!"

They turned into White Horse Close. There was no

tavern here now, only apartments. The inn had gone long ago. The close opened out into a wide courtyard and in daytime had more light than most. It was one of the prettiest in the Old Town, with its baskets and window boxes of flowers, not blooming at this time of year, of course, but in summer making a fine show. It was night-time now. Some of the windows were dark; others showed light at the edges of their curtains.

Somewhere here was the apartment given in 1796 to Ranald Cunningham by the mysterious nobleman known only as Lamont. There were several doors. Which one was it? They went round reading the names on the plates, but beside a few of the bells there were none at all. Some people obviously did not like to advertise themselves.

"We could try ringing them," suggested Lucy.

"It's a bit late to do that."

"Not too late. It's not quite ten yet. Most people would be up."

"Trouble is, even if we did manage to ring Dad's, he might not answer."

"Let's try a couple anyway."

Lucy pressed one and got no response. She tried another and this time a woman's voice came booming out of the grille to demand, "Yes? What do you want?"

"We're looking for a Mr Ranald Cunningham."

"Never heard of him."

"Probably nobody has," said Will, "not if he's using the place as a secret hideaway."

They wandered around looking at the windows, which revealed nothing.

"We can't give up now," said Lucy. "Even if we have to camp down here till he comes out."

"I can't see us being allowed to do that!"

A man and woman were entering the close.

"Let's ask them." Lucy went forward to meet them and Will followed.

The couple looked at them slightly askance.

"We're looking for a Mr Ranald Cunningham," said Lucy.

"Don't know anyone of that name," replied the woman. "Do you, Donald?"

He shook his head.

"Does he live here?" asked the woman.

"Well, yes, some of the time."

"He's six feet tall," put in Will "and he's got dark hair with just a little bit of grey at the sides."

The woman frowned. "Sounds a bit like our mystery man, doesn't it, Donald?"

"Mystery man?" echoed Lucy.

"Yes, he has the next flat to ours. He seems to come and go, always on his own. He's been around more recently. Never has much to say for himself."

"It might be him," said Will.

"Could you let us in the outside door?" asked Lucy "Just so that we could find out."

"You can ring the bell," said the man. "It's that one on the right."

Lucy rang but no one answered.

"He was in earlier. I'm sure I heard him."

"Perhaps if we were to knock on his inside door?" said Lucy.

"You can come in with us and try if you think it will do any good."

The couple unlocked the door and went ahead of them up the stairs to the first floor. "That's his flat there," said the woman, indicating it.

The couple waited in the doorway of their own apartment, which made it difficult for them. Lucy and Will realised that they probably wanted to make sure that they were not up to anything. The trouble was that if you were a teenager people thought you must be!

There was no name on the door they were facing, and no bell. After a moment's hesitation, Will raised his fist and knocked. It was very quiet. There didn't appear to be any movement on the other side of the door.

Will knocked again and Lucy, forgetting about the onlookers, cried out, "Dad, it's us! Will and Lucy. Please open the door. *Please!* We want to see you."

They waited, scarcely daring to breathe. Lucy had her fingers crossed tightly. Then they heard a chain being unhooked, and the door opened. And there stood their father!

"Dad!" they cried, launching themselves at him.

He hugged them fiercely and when at length they separated they saw that he had tears in his eyes.

"Come in." He opened the door wide. They went in and he closed it behind them.

The living room was as William and Louisa had described it, except that the sofa could not have survived for over two hundred years. At some time somebody had replaced it but the table looked old and scored, as did the two upright wooden chairs. They could imagine William and Louisa sitting there. A wood fire burned in the grate, making the place warm and cosy.

"How did you manage to find me?" asked their father, sounding incredulous that they had.

They told him about finding the journal.

"That was clever of you." He said he'd been planning for some time to tell them about it, and this place, very soon. His father had brought him here when he was their age.

"The family's secret hideaway!" said Lucy.

"My father told me it had to be a secret and that I,

in turn, should let my heir into it when he or she – or both of you! – reached your teens."

"So that's why Mum doesn't know about it," said Will.

"Yes, I've always felt a bit awkward about that."

"Perhaps we'll have to tell her now?"

"I think we shall." Their dad then started to say how terribly sorry and ashamed he was to have put them through such an ordeal. "I'll never forgive myself."

"You have to!" Lucy hated to hear him sound so sad.

He shook his head. "I just seemed to freak out. Everything was in such a horrible stupid mess and was going from bad to worse."

What was amazing them was how *normal* he seemed. They couldn't believe it. He was the dad they'd always known and they'd expected to find him in a heap.

Paper and pen lay on the table. It looked as if he had been making notes.

"Sit down," he said.

They took the sofa and he sat on one of the upright chairs.

"How's your mum?" he asked first of all.

"OK," said Will.

"Coping," added Lucy.

Their father nodded. "I'm sure she is." He smiled. "I've been trying to. I guess you realise I had a kind of breakdown? That's how it felt, like I was breaking down. Into tiny little pieces. So I came to hide. Not very noble, is it?"

"It doesn't *matter*, Dad," insisted Lucy.

"It does actually, Lucy. Because it affected the two of you and your mum. The first few days I was here I was in a kind of pit of black despair. Then I went and talked to the doctor and he referred me to a counsellor. That was what I needed. Somebody to talk things through with. Before that I'd felt I was peering into a tunnel blocked off at the end."

A piece of wood tumbled out of the fire on to the grate and he got up to put it back.

"The result is I've been able to take some decisions. I think I've found a way forward, to make a new start."

"That's great," said Will.

"But what about the money you owe?" asked Lucy. "Will you be able to pay that?" Without their house being sold, she was thinking, but did not voice.

"I'm going to have to sell this flat, I'm afraid. I hate the idea, but I've got to."

"Oh, Dad!" cried Lucy. To think that they had just found this lovely little hideaway which had been Louisa and William's before them and were going to lose it before they'd had a chance to use it!

"I know. I feel dreadful about it. Especially since my father – and grandfather – made me solemnly promise to never ever sell it. And when I promised I truly thought I never would." Their father's voice cracked and he put his back to them and stared out of the window. A few flakes of snow had begun to fall. "I shall be betraying their trust. They explained to me how it had been handed down through the family for generations. To think that *I* should be the one to break the chain!"

"You can't help it!" cried Lucy, wanting to get up and comfort him, yet sensing he needed to be left alone for the moment.

"I should have been able to." He turned to face them again. "I was a fool, an absolute fool. I ran up all those debts. If my father knew—"

"But he doesn't," said Lucy. Their grandfather had died before they were born.

"We don't mind that you can't pass it on to us," said Will, though he did feel a pang as he said it. "Are you able to sell it?"

"I've been into it with the solicitor. There's a clause in the will which states that if a member of the family should find himself in dire need – especially in debt – he may do so. I've thought and thought and I just can't see any other way out."

"It's OK, Dad." Lucy was worried that he might slump into another breakdown. "Like Will says, we don't mind, really we don't."

"It is only an old flat," said Will.

"There are a few days left before your case comes up in court," said Lucy.

"Do you think you could manage to sell it before then?" asked Will.

"The solicitor already has a buyer ready to sign on the dotted line and with the money in cash. He could have sold it ten times over apparently." Their father looked round. "It is a little gem," he said sadly. "I'm so sorry, children, that I won't be able to pass on your inheritance."

"We still have our house," Lucy pointed out. "It's not as if we're homeless," she added, thinking of poor old Peg.

Will's mobile rang. "It's Mum," he said, looking at the number on the display.

"Tell her we're coming home," said their father.

When they reached the house they let him go ahead and spend a few minutes alone with their mother. When they did go in they saw that she had been crying. They did not feel far from it themselves. Lucy had been sniffling all the way up the hill.

"We should have a special meal to celebrate, Mum," she said.

"We were just going to have fish fingers!" said their mother ruefully. "I didn't have time to shop today."

"Why don't we have a carry-out?" suggested their father.

"I suppose we could." Their mother was hesitating a little, thinking, they knew, of the money. "OK, why not?" She fetched her purse.

Will and Lucy went out to buy it. They were told they could choose. Lucy wanted Chinese, Will Indian. In the end they opted for Thai, which was kind of in between. While they were waiting for the order to be made up they talked about the family's little hideaway.

"It's a shame it has to be sold," sighed Lucy. "It'd have been a great place to hang out in."

"Better to have Dad home, though."

There was no question about that and it was wonderful that he was going to be able to clear his debts. But what about afterwards? Even if there was some money left over from the sale of the flat it wouldn't last all that long. He would have to get a job, wouldn't he? Their mum didn't get paid a huge amount at the library.

When they brought the carry-out home they found their parents sitting together on the settee drinking a glass of red wine. Their dad had his arm round their mum's shoulder. He looked as if he had never been away.

"Your dad's got another piece of news for you," said their mother. "There'll be a little money left over from the sale of the flat."

Will and Lucy looked at each other. Surely he wasn't going to start up another of his business enterprises! It might be the end of Gran if he did.

"He's going to use it to do a teacher-training course."

Their dad would make a great teacher, they knew that. He already had a degree in history and from the time they were very young he had told them stories about the past and brought the people and places to life.

"That's a great idea," said Will.

"Fantastic," said Lucy.

Chapter 22

Louisa and William

Since we have Papa home again this will be the last entry in our journal so we are writing it together.

There was great rejoicing in our house when we brought Papa in. We had to fetch Maman's smelling salts, of course, but she recovered quickly. Bessie picked up her skirts and did a little jig in the middle of the kitchen floor. The two of them were even more delighted when they heard that Papa's debts had been cleared *and* he had some money in hand as well.

"No more running down the street on the stroke of Sunday midnight," he said, his face beaming.

"You must run to the flesher's, Bessie," cried our mother. "*Vite, vite!* Buy a guineafowl and a leg of mutton and a dozen fresh eggs. Tonight we feast!"

We looked at each other, the same thought spinning through our heads. How long would the money last? And what would we do when it ran out? Papa could not be allowed to get into debt again.

As if he could read our minds, he said, "Don't worry, children, I have a plan. A way to earn a living. Perhaps not a big one, but a living nevertheless."

He had had plans before but none of them had ever worked out.

"You are not going to write another book, I hope?" said our mother. "I mean to say, I do not mind you write the book, but the last one still lies in the drawer unseen by the world."

"I have hopes that it may be seen some day, but no, it was not of that I was thinking. While I was lodging in the palace an old friend came to visit me. Do you remember James Christie? He lives up in Buccleuch Place."

"You seemed to have much social life in the abbey."

"Let Papa tell us, Maman," we begged.

"We studied together at the university, James and I. He teaches in the High School. He came to tell me that there was a vacancy for the teaching of language and literature and he had recommended me for the position. I have applied and been accepted."

"Bravo!" we cried.

"A schoolmaster will not earn much," lamented our mother. "We will never move to the New Town now."

"*Maman!*" we cried.

"I am pleased, of course," she went on hurriedly. "I am glad you will have employment, Ranald. It is *merveilleux*! But I wish for your sake that it could be something better. You deserve more."

"It could not be better," he declared. "I shall enjoy teaching the boys."

Papa is a good teacher. We can vouch for that. He makes everything he talks about interesting.

"And you, William," he said, "will come with me to the school as a pupil. I am sorry, Louisa, that you will not be able to but, as you know, it is a school for boys only. I think we might send you to Miss Smith's Academy for young ladies."

We are sad to think that we shall be parted for our education since we never have been before. We have learned everything we know together and are used to having each other's company from morning till night. One consolation is that Charlotte is to be enrolled at Miss Smith's Academy also. She had told us so the previous week.

We went out to help Bessie with the errands as there would be too much for her to carry. Papa gave her a purseful of money before we left. She was happy that she could settle all our outstanding bills around the town, and so were we. We could look the shopkeepers in the eye again. We met up with Peg and were able to give her a bannock and cheese and a salt herring that we purchased from a Newhaven fishwife.

Afterwards we called on Charlotte and told her our news, though not the part about the apartment, our secret hideaway. For that has to remain a family secret. She was pleased to know that she had been of help by telling us about Monsieur Goriot going to play whist with the count and Madame de Polastron. It was the bit of the jigsaw that had helped complete the picture.

We had our feast this evening and Bessie sat at table with us, supping wine and becoming a little tiddly.

Papa proposed a toast. "To a new beginning," he said, raising his glass.

We are pleased that we can conclude the story of our father as an 'abbey laird', though sad to lay the journal aside. It has come to seem like a friend during our time of trouble. We have decided to place it in the wall cavity in the sitting room in the hope that, sometime in the future, one of our descendants – or perhaps two, for twins do run in our family – may discover it and find our tale of interest.

Chapter 23

So the other Ranald Cunningham became a teacher as their own father was to do!

"I guess a number of things run in the family," said Will with a grin.

"I wonder what became of the Comte d'Artois," said Lucy.

"Let's find out."

They rummaged through some of their father's history books until they found a reference to the Comte d'Artois. They looked it up.

The count had become King Charles X of France in 1824, following the death of his brother Louis XVIII, and had reigned for six years until being forced to abdicate after yet another revolution. So, in 1830, once again in debt and fleeing from creditors, he returned to seek refuge in the sanctuary of Holyrood Abbey for another two years.

"He didn't seem to learn a lesson," said Lucy. She hoped their dad would!

By 1830, William and Louisa would have been nearly fifty years old. Lucy and Will could not imagine them grown-up and middle-aged. They could think of them only as being of a similar age to themselves, tailing the evil Monsieur Goriot down the hill into the Grassmarket.

They reread the closing paragraph of the journal and afterwards turned back to the front page to look again at the sign of the black dagger, drawn by their ancestors more than two hundred years before. It was time then to close the book, rewrap it in oilcloth, and return it to its place in the wall.

"I shall miss William and Louisa," said Lucy.

"We can always read their story again," said Will.